I0547951

Jaded
By Sydney Trager

This book is dedicated to anyone
who has ever had a dream so crazy
they've had to write it down
somewhere. Thanks to my family
and friends for supporting me.

"Our dreams are so related though they're often underestimated." –Jack Johnson

Chapter 1 [Lily]

They want to write a story about me. They want me to go on national television and talk about the book. Or not book, journal I guess. They want me to talk on and on about the book, but the truth is, I know just as much as they do. I don't know why I have it; I don't know why it's in my house. I've read it over and over and over again, but anyone can read. They want me to publish the journal, so everyone can know what happened. They would give me credit in the beginning, saying something like "In honor of Lily Dorlin, we wouldn't be able to read this piece of history without her," but I don't think I can accept that. Credit for what? I'm not related to the book, at least I don't think I am, and I'm not even entirely sure it's real. I guess it's got to be, considering everyone's making such a big deal about it.

None of this would have happened if it weren't for Colby. It's hard to be mad when he's so good looking, but I'm definitely not happy. I'm just glad he didn't say anything about the map at the beginning. If the reporters could get their hands on the map, they'd know where the legendary crystal once was. But that was Jade's favorite part of her home, and I almost feel like I need to protect it for her. She'd want the crystal to be honored, and if word got out of its' location, they'd go straight over and take apart anything and everything that is left. Colby might have given the reporters my secret, but he didn't give them all of it.

I don't regret showing him the book, and I don't even regret trusting him with this secret, I get it, it's kind of a big deal and probably needed to be exposed anyways, but maybe I just didn't want to be the one to deal with it. I could've passed it down to one of my kids and maybe they would know what to do. They'd probably get the confidence from their father because that's a trait I most certainly lack.

I'm thinking about my future children when my cell phone rings AGAIN. Who could it be this time?

NBC? Dateline? Maybe it'd be Sylvia. I really hoped it would. She goes to my school, and I'm pretty close to her. Well, she may not think we're as close as I do. She's really popular; friends with everyone. Maybe that's why she's friends with me, because she pities me. She says she thinks I'm interesting because I've lived in so many places, and she loves to travel. It's not like I've lived in exotic places though so I don't really understand what she means, but I love having more friends! Especially because I don't have many. Maybe Sylvia heard I was being bombarded by these TV people, and she wanted to check in. That would be really sweet.

Oh, wait, it's Colby. To pick up or not to pick up? I mean this is the boy I've been secretly crushing on since I moved here, but he is also the one who caused this stupid mess. Who am I kidding? I'm picking up.

"Hello?" Cool, sultry but calm. He probably thinks I'm good with all of this drama.

"Lily! Don't hang up! I'm sorry to be doing this to you. Can I come over? I know it's probably not easy and TRUST ME I didn't realize telling my dad about your book would cause all of this!"

"Colby, your dad's an anchor on the *Today Show*. He can make anything a big deal. And it's not my book, I think it's Jade's book. Or maybe it was given to Storm. Either way, it's not mine."

"God Lily, I'm tired of explaining this to you. This is not a normal book, and this is not a normal situation. This piece of journalism you happened to have been hoarding as a bedtime story is the story behind the Lost Land, or what's the real name? País de los Sueños? This wouldn't just fall into the wrong hands, whether you're happy about it or not you've got something to do with the book. I'm coming over, no objections. I got you into this, I'm going to help you through it."

And with that he hung up. That's what I love about Colby. I moved here just two years ago, but he acts like we've been best friends forever. To tell you the truth, I've always felt that way too. I remember when I first got here, and though I'd been used to moving since my dad's boss keeps relocating us, I was nervous about this place. I was starting high school after all, which is a big deal, and dad said this would be the final house I'd have before college. It was in New York City though, which I'd always heard about, everywhere I lived.

This place was special, and I really understood that when I saw our apartment. Dad told me that in New York he had a better position at his company so he was earning more. I didn't really need an excuse. My new home was a beautiful, open, modern space. I had a huge room with a chair hanging from the ceiling and my own TV. Down the hall was my dad's room, which was probably double the size of mine. We both had these over the top bathrooms with showers that were as big as my kitchen in my old house and the whole apartment had a touch screen system that controlled it. You could play music throughout the entire apartment with the speaker system, or chose just one room. I not only wanted to stay in one place for once, but I wanted to stay at *this* place.

But back to Colby. When I went to the new student orientation at Northern Court High School everyone was assigned a buddy to help you through the first few weeks. It was girl with girl or boy with boy, I guess to make it more relatable. Anyways, I got there late of course, and there was only one buddy left. The teachers kind of freaked when they learned I was a girl, because Colby was already there and ready to tour me. He was a little shocked too. It's probably because of my name.

My real name is Ryan Lily Dorlin. My mom named me Ryan because someone extremely close to her was named Ryan too. She clearly didn't think about the fact that I'm a girl, and Ryan's a boy's name. But I like it, because that's one of the only things I know about her. I have my name and my stupid book. Dad doesn't really like to talk about her so

I can't even really say I have memories or stories. I do know the only thing she really did while I was alive was name me, stay for a year, and leave.

Somewhere in between then she put the book in a box in my room. Every time we moved, so did the box, and when I was eight I found it. We never fully unpacked because some of our moves lasted all of six months, but when I was living in Washington I got bored one day and started to look through every single box. It was one of the last ones that held this worn out leather journal. There was an envelope in it too, a beautiful lilac color that said Ryan on it. I think she'd be disappointed to know I go by my middle name: Lily. However, I was disappointed when she left without a trace and never looked back. So disappointed, I'd never read the letter. Maybe it wasn't my disappointment that was keeping me away, it was fear, but whatever it was, I wasn't ready to open it.

I like the name Lily better, it's girly, and if I don't even know the meaning behind Ryan, I feel no need to use it. But using my middle name can be confusing, which is why I ended up with Colby at the orientation. I guess they didn't read the middle name when they were assigning buddies for the orientation.

They insisted if I could just come back the next day I would have a real buddy; a girl buddy. I looked at Colby who kind of looked bummed at how easily they were blowing him off. I learned later he was just happy to be considered a leader and now because they screwed up he wouldn't have been. He also said he thought I seemed cool because my name was throwing the teachers off, and that made me unique. I told them I was fine, and I really was. I stood in the red and black painted hallway and explained how I always move, and how I'm used to making new friends. One of the cool teachers who still happens to be my favorite, Mr. C, calmed everyone down and let me go with Colby.

I'll never forget the way Colby smiled when the situation was resolved. His turquoise blue eyes that pretty much any female could get lost in lit up and that was when everything changed, or began. It created this bond, like he was really psyched to be with me, and he could tell after that I was pretty psyched to be with him. It could have been just because of my "cool" name, or maybe because he was finally acknowledged as a "leader," but I like to believe it was just me. It was just this thing that passed between us, I can't describe what it was, but it made my whole body feel electrified. I'd like to believe it was the same for him.

Colby and I did the usual getting to know each other, but the thing that was different this time was unlike the rest of my encounters as the new kid, I could tell Colby was listening and he cared. I could tell him I played soccer in second grade, and he wasn't just going to throw that information away, he would remember it. In fact, I knew he was taking it all in, because he's never one to forget, which I've learned the hard way. Basically anything I've ever said, he keeps locked away in his private bank of knowledge and doesn't fail to bring it up in conversation.

This, of course, has gotten me into trouble. Like when I told him that I lived in California for eight years and surfed all day instead of going to school. Should've known that one would bite me in the butt. Dad quickly shot my lie down with a laugh as I turned bright red with embarrassment. Every moment similar to that is always scary to me. I don't know why someone as good looking and amazing as Colby is even giving me the time of day, let alone being my best friend, and I always feel like any mess up I make could be the end. I know it's stupid, and trust me, he's told me a hundred times that it's ridiculous, but I've never really had a reason to believe that I deserve someone like him. My mom definitely didn't make me feel like I deserve anyone at all, and my dad's always working so not many deep chats about my confidence have ever happened.

Colby's at the door. Ugh. The way he flips his hair and smiles as if he's got everything to be happy about, even when he's alone, just kills me. I guess he does have a lot of reasons to be happy. Everyone in school loves him, his mom is beautiful and kind, his father is famous and loving, and he's got this amazing older brother. He's never had a girlfriend though, and trust me, this is the biggest mystery. Bigger than the book, and how I came across it. Like, he's perfect. Even the way he just walks in, he hugs me, and he looks at me like he's so concerned. He's truly sorry for what he did, and I'm not even mad.

"Colby, it's okay."

"It's not, Lily. You trusted me. I didn't even think about telling my family, but I shouldn't have been telling anyone at all. Your entire life is going to change because I couldn't keep a secret."

Whoa. If you put it that way…

"It's not your fault! I mean it is, but I'm not blaming you. I still trust you. I guess I should have known this was going to happen anyway."

"Well, what are you going to do? Are you going to go on TV? Are you going to let them publish it?"

"I have no idea."

And I start crying. Just like that. I don't even know why. Maybe because I've always felt like this was a secret that my mom and I shared. The only one we ever have, and will share. Or maybe because I have no idea what I'm getting myself into. I've read the book, but it doesn't mean I know about it, or where it came from, or why I have it. I don't feel like I can go talk about it for hours and hours, when anybody else could just read it and know exactly what I know. Colby's so awesome. He's just hugging me. He knows I always feel way worse when I have to talk while I'm crying, so he's letting this one play out. And it's not like I'm feeling awkward in the silence, it's actually really nice.

"Colby, what should I do?"

"I think you should figure out your own stuff before you start sharing it with the world. We should look more into this book."

"We can't look into it, it hasn't exactly been put out to the public yet, hence my problem."

"We can figure out anything that anyone has ever known about the Lost Land, and we can try and figure out why you have it. Have you ever tried asking your dad?"

Colby doesn't know what happened to my mom. He doesn't know anything about her. He doesn't even know she's the one who left me the book. He just knows not to ask or even bring her up.

"No, the only thing I know is that my mom left it for me, and can we start calling it País de los Sueños, I mean that's the real name of the Lost Land after all."

He's excited.

"Well, that's pretty awesome Lily. If we find her, I'm sure she could tell you everything we need to know about the book. She's our key to success!"

At least I thought he knew never to ask about her.

"Don't you think I've been trying to find her?"

I honestly haven't been trying. I used to, when I was little, but I was stupid and careless. I guess I could do it now, but the subject kind of tires me out.

"But I can help! It would make it easier!"

"If you're dead set on this, fine. But even if we do find her, I'm pretty sure the book would not be first thing we'd talk about would not be the book."

"I'm patient. Lily, you're the best! I know it's hard to deal with your mom and all, but we'll do it together! I got to go back home now, Dad's still kind of freaking out."

He kisses me on the cheek and leaves. AH! I mean it's not the first time he's kissed me on the cheek, but still, it's not getting old any time soon. And, I just agreed to find my mom. Now I'm really in over my head. God help me.

Chapter 2 [Jade]

Dear Revista,

I'm naming you Revista because I don't want to call this a diary. Diaries are for seven-year-olds who have crushes on boys in class. I'm fifteen, and I don't go to class, so this is not a diary. Instead, I'm homeschooled by my parents. Revista means journal in Spanish and a journal seems a little more age appropriate. My mom and dad gave me this journal for my birthday, yesterday. Fifteen is not one of those ages that would make you be excited about, not sixteen or twenty-five or fifty, but I was excited.

Being homeschooled, and living on this island can get kind of boring honestly. The journal was pretty much exactly what I needed. It may seem cool to live in País de los Sueños, because it's a remote island off of Mexico, but I'm starting to let my brain wander. I don't have that much to do anymore, I've pretty much explored every inch of the island. My parents are always busy and I've explored every inch of this island a thousand times. I don't have that many people to hang out with either. I used to go to a normal school, but I stopped that a while ago, and it didn't take long for the other kids to forget about me. My only friends have been the people I see in the park, and the market.

The Rochella park is the place where the crystal is. It's kind of far away from my house, but the island is small, so it's never a problem to get anywhere. Ever since my parents took me to Rochella's rolling green hills with the wildly colorful trees that stand and watch over the citizens, I've been mesmerized by the iridescent glow of the crystal. Mom and Dad explained to me pretty early on the entire story of the land, and I was so enthused that this beautiful monument in front of me could be in charge of what happens here. It seems like every day there's something new and exciting about the crystal, and it's not just the change in color. The crystal portrays the status of our dreams from the past night. The more vivid the dream, the brighter the crystal. There is a

*whole color system too, kind of like a
mood ring. It changes by the subject
and vibe of the overall dreams.*

*Today the crystal is a brilliant
emerald green. Clearly, last night
the dreams were about power. This
could be different for everyone. On
our island, we don't really have a
dictatorship or a government, we all
just get along. We don't have many
decisions to be made and when we
do we usually don't even know about
it, because the fairies deal with it.
Maybe people were dreaming about
having a powerful position, like a
king or queen. For me, power would
be fulfillment. Ever since I turned
fourteen, I've started to feel like
something is missing. I've never been
anywhere other then País de los
Sueños, and I know there is so much
more for me to see. Dad taught me
about all of the different places in
geography. I want to travel around,
but for some reason no one here
really leaves. It makes sense since
other places make their citizens work
for money, and then they use the
money to buy things like a house,
food, and clothing. That's not the*

way it is here. As long as the crystal is glowing, life goes on. We have a market, where people make clothes, food, and materials that everyone needs. You don't have to pay ever. It may sound confusing, but the dream fairies supply everything we need.

The fairies, or hadas, are beautiful creatures here on our island. They seem so fragile and innocent, yet they pretty much run my homeland. All of them have gorgeously big eyes that just stare at you. I guess you could call them observers, because that's all they really do. They observe and collect the dreams and bring them to the crystal so it can glow. They also glow. The hadas have medium sized bodies but large and delicate wings that stretch out when they fly. If there is ever a hada in sight, you would know because of the sparkling aura that whispers off of them.

A lot of what the hadas do goes unexplained. They give the workers in the market material for clothing, food for cooking, and tools for houses, though no one knows where

*they get those things. Not many
question it though, we're all happy,
why should we wonder? When you
first move here, the Hadas show you
where you're going to live, and give
you a tour of the town. They're like
the information booth you go to, so
you know where to go and what to
see. The most powerful hada is
called Pajana. Pajana is considered
the king of the hadas, and I rarely
see him. He mostly stays inside,
making decisions. He's known as the
brains behind everything they do,
similar to the queen bee in a beehive.
Pajana is a brilliant red color, which
is my favorite. Most of the hadas are
yellow, green, purple, pink, and blue.
Pajana is the only red I've ever seen.
He'd never be the one to greet
anyone when they move here though,
most people live here a few years
before they meet him. After the hadas
show you around, you're most likely
going to end up with my parents.*

*Mom and dad teach a class on
lucid dreaming. After all, dreaming
is the most important thing you can
do in País de los Sueños. It's good to
learn how to lucid dream first,*

because then you'll be able to control your dreams, and make sure that they're intricate and positive. It really doesn't matter what you dream about, it's just important you're having vivid and positive dreams. It's funny because when people come here they always say that this is paradise; this is what they dream about. They wonder what we could be dreaming about if we have everything we need right here.

It's true this island is beautiful. Sometimes I take that for granted because it's all I've ever known, and when tourists come have conversations with me I truly understand how lucky I am. They marvel at the vegetation here. It rains when it needs to, leaving us with lush green leaves on every tree you see. We don't have seasons, we just have warm weather. The sun beats down pretty heavily, but if you're ever overheated you can just jump into the crystal clear ocean. I like to think the salt in the water is just more of the hada's sparkling glow. Everyone says our island is enchanted, and I think it's partly because of the way the water sparkles. We've got hundreds of different kinds of fish swimming around, all of them vibrantly colored, and because the water is so clear, you're always bound to see them. If you swim out deep enough you'll see dolphins.

I used to have one dolphin I really loved when I was about 9. I named her Star because her blowhole had been damaged by a sea urchin and was shaped like a star. We swam together every morning, before I would have school or I'd have to go to the market. I would hold on to her strong fin and we'd glide through the oceans together. But Star started to get sick, I could tell, because she was weaker. By the end it was more like I was pulling her instead of her pulling me. One morning, Star didn't come. I knew. That day I built a small memorial out of seashells on the shore. I searched miles of the beach to find the most ornate ones I could; Star deserved it. I sat by my sculpture and wept for my dear friend and the rest of the dolphins leapt in the air far away, signaling they were also mourning our beloved Star.

I dream about her sometimes. The tourists make it seem like my life is perfect, but everyone has problems. That's why mom and dad teach lucid dreaming, so we can control our dreams and make them positive. After learning lucid dreaming, there is no such thing as a nightmare, and País de los Sueños has no room for nightmares. Nightmares would mess up the crystal, and would upset the dream fairies. Luckily, that's never happened before. Well, actually that's not completely true.

Now, it's only a myth, but I still believe it. There's a rumor that before I was born, a mysterious man that came to town. Though he tried and tried, he couldn't dream. It wasn't even that he was having nightmares, he just wasn't dreaming at all. I don't even know if that's possible. No matter how many people tried to teach him, he just couldn't do it. There were many conferences within the hadas and at the final conference they invited the man to join them. I'm not sure what happened at the conference, no one is, but the next day the man disappeared.

Everyone thinks he killed himself because he was so ashamed. I don't know what to think.

When I was younger and went to school with other kids, we used to talk about it in the hallways. None of the adults ever let us say anything, so we always had to whisper. You can imagine how hard it would be to get a real story when you've got a ton of little kids whispering about something that none of us were even around for. Every time any of the teachers heard, they'd freak out and make us stop talking about it.

Everyone thought it was because it was one of those things that could make you have nightmares, but I think it's because they know it's true. I can't even ask my parents about it because we constantly have people milling around, learning new techniques of dreaming. When I get those few and special moments alone with them, we don't exactly talk about the story that the entire town hides.

I once asked them about it when I was younger,

"Why couldn't you guys teach that man how to dream? I thought you could teach anyone how to dream."

"What man?" My mom asked, barely even looking up at me.

"Mom, you know what I'm talking about. The mystery man. The one that couldn't dream."

She looked up at me, and something in her face was different. She basically has a smile plastered on her face since she starts class with my dad. It's warm and inviting, and it's something I've always loved about her. Yes, sometimes my mom is really busy teaching others to dream instead of paying attention to me, but whenever I see her, I see that smile, and it makes me feel right at home. Unfortunately, she didn't smile when

I asked her about the man. Instead, her eyes got darker, and her tone was grave.

"Honey, go get ready for dinner. I don't know what you think you know, but it's nothing we need to be discussing."

That was the end of that. I know something bizarre happened, or at least that some of the story is true, because if it weren't, my mom would have laughed, and called me her little "soñador," or dreamer, since she thinks I have the biggest imagination in País de los Sueños. They're so proud of me here, I'm good at dreaming and I have a place, but I'm starting to feel like there's something more for me.

Ugh, dad is calling for me. Time for math class. How do they expect me to think about trigonometry when I'm still stuck in a fog about the mystery man, I've decided I want to travel the world but I have no way of leaving País de los Sueños, and last night the town dreamed about power, but I still don't feel like I have any?

Well, I guess all of those things will have to be put on hold, since multiplication and division are calling my name.

Until then,

Jade

Chapter 3

I'm just scared. I'm scared of the knocks that keep banging down my door. I'm scared of the countless phone calls I keep getting. I'm scared of leaving to go to school, walking through the cameras and reporters that wait outside my building. I wish my dad were here to protect me, but he's off to another exotic country, writing another exciting story. I think it's Indonesia this time, I'm not sure, but I know it's somewhere I can't contact him very easily, so I'm trying to deal with this on my own.

Colby's helping me, too. He picks me up in the morning before school and walks me home. He hangs out with me when he's not playing sports, or tutoring freshman at the tutor center. When we're together I'm not as scared; he holds off the media, he picks up the phone and tells off the reporters, and he never lets me watch the news.

I'm not the most popular girl in school, I've never been the lead in a play, I've never been involved in a scandal. Honestly, I've never really had to experience any attention on myself, unless it's the occasional, "Who is this new kid?" situation, but that dies down pretty quickly. To see myself on the news would terrify me, and I most certainly wouldn't know how to handle it, which is why I've been staying away from watching it.

I understand the situation I'm in completely. I understand that the whole world has always heard about an island off of Mexico, and I understand that no one knows anything about it. They don't even know the name, which is why they call it the Lost Land. They know it exists, they know it's special, but no one's actually ever been there, at least in recent history. People try all of the time, but no one has ever come back with a story to tell, which makes the whole mystery even more interesting.

I also understand the fact that I have the key behind the entire history. Jade's journal tells the story of the land, of what it is now, and what it was. And I know it seems crazy I'm not sharing it with the rest of the world, but this is just so confusing for me. For one thing, this was a gift from my mom, the mom who I don't even remember. So, how am I supposed to trust this is the real story? This could be a story she made up. I wouldn't know the difference. Another thing is that this is the only thing I have with her, and maybe she left it with me in trust. Trusting that I wouldn't share it with the world, wouldn't expose Jade and Storm and their family to everyone who has been in the dark this whole time. I mean, is there a reason that País de los Sueños is being kept a secret? If so, I wouldn't want to mess everything up.

And what's the point? If the whole world knows about it, it'll probably just become another vacation spot for well off families. They wouldn't respect the beauty of it unless they felt the emotion in Jade's words, and there's no telling whether they would. If the Lost Land has been "The Lost Land" for so long, maybe it should remain that way.

Colby's dad wants me to release it. Then again, it would be amazing ratings for him, and a huge boost in his career. Does he even care about País de los Sueños?

Then there's Colby, who wants me to release it, but doesn't want me to unless I'm ready. And that means finding my mom.

My mom's a big part of this too. I know the majority of the world would love it if I put this journal out to the public, so all of them could read it. It seems like it would make sense for me to follow the majority. But the majority has nothing on the opinion of my mom. And that's confusing too, I know, because she abandoned me, so why should I care so much? But what if she forgot this book, and she didn't even mean leave it for me, and I was never supposed to have read it? Or what if I release it and it's just a story she wrote, and then everyone believes it and she gets in trouble for credibility issues, and she hates me? I have to know what she wants. If she wants it out, I'll call Colby's dad first, I leave it all to him. But I will not compromise the only piece of relationship I have with her; I'm hanging on to a thin wire but it's all I have.

Chapter 4

Dear Revista,

How come in math the numbers always add up, or there's always solutions? That's not the way it is in real life. I know it's stupid for me to still be thinking about the mystery of the man who couldn't dream, but what else is there to do? I could spend time thinking about my future, but I have no idea what it's going to look like, and it scares me. Where will I be? Though I yearn to leave País de los Sueños, I have a feeling this will forever be my home. I don't want to make it look like I hate it here, because I don't. I have great parents, a beautiful home, a good education, and a lively imagination that is constantly complimented because of it's importance here. Life is simple.

And there's something else that I like here. Not something, someone. I sound pretty stupid considering the fact that I don't know this guy at all, but I feel like I've known him

*forever. I guess I should explain.
Yesterday, after math, dad wanted
me to get food. He said we were
having a guest for dinner, so I
needed to pick up a few things.*

*Everything was going exactly
how it usually does. We always have
people staying with us, fascinated by
my parents and their work, and I end
up picking stuff up, because they're
busy, or because they know I love
walking through the park. I went to
Melinda, my parents' favorite food
teller. Melinda is basically a second
mom to me, she always looks out for
me because she knows my parents
can't. She has the best bread in all of
the market, but she always saves
some for me before it is all gone. We
were talking about the color of the
crystal and I was picking out which
bread I wanted, when I saw a flash
out of the corner of my eye.*

*I felt like someone was
watching me, but when I turned
around no one was there. So I went
back to the bread, but I saw the flash
again, and this time I was prepared.
I whipped around and saw a boy, my*

age, looking at me curiously. For a split second we made eye contact, and it was almost like he was the missing piece to my puzzle, and he knew it. Then, without warning, he was gone.

I finished getting the food but my mind kept going back to that boy. I wanted to know his name, his favorite color, where he was from, what he was doing here, what he does in his spare time; anything and everything. It's true that I'm always looking for more friends since going to school means staying in my room with either my dad or mom, and the kids I used to go to school with kind of stopped caring about me and moved on with their lives. But this wasn't the usual curiosity I feel when I see someone new. Because even though he was new, it seemed like I've always known him, like he's always been a part of me. I desperately needed to find out more about him. That's why I was so thrilled to go home. I knew that if he just moved here, he was most likely enrolled in my parents' class, and I wanted to know everything I could about him. I was practically running home, I was so excited.

I burst into the door, threw the basket of food on the table, and ran to find my parents, who already had their guest seated in the living room. Normally, I'm polite, and introduce myself, but at that moment, I felt like my issue was more important then my manners.

"I need to know all of the new people that have signed up for your classes. There's this boy that just moved here, and I think he's my age, and I want to know what his name is."

I really wish I had just sucked it up and showed some manners. If I had, I wouldn't have completely embarassed myself.

"Jade, honey, aren't you going to introduce yourself to our guest?"

The fact that mom called me "honey" in front of him. I could kill her. And yes, that's right, as soon as I finished my rant of wishing to get to know the new kid, he, himself, stood up and turned around from the couch. He turned red, and looked shocked, like I had just given away his deepest secret. It's almost like he thought he'd never see me again.

"This is our daughter, Jade."

Dad said, clearly covering for me, since I was trying to pick my jaw up from the floor. Man, this kid was cute. He had dirty blond hair that was colored from the sun, and long eyelashes surrounding his big, hazel eyes. He was tall too, definitely taller then me, and he had full, peach colored lips. I think he was analyzing me just as much as I was analyzing him.

"Jade, this is Storm Brandick. He just moved here, and he's fifteen-years-old. He's going to be living with us, and going to school with you, so hopefully you two get along. And what were you saying about looking at who joined my classes?"

"Nothing, never mind."

WHAT? Storm. First of all, that is the coolest name ever. It makes him edgy, and mysterious. Second of all, he's going to be living with me? And going to school with me? Is this real? My parents have never had anyone else live with us, not even like a nanny or a cleaning lady. And where are his parents? I know I should be really happy that this really great looking guy is moving in with me, but I'm way too curious to think about that.

"Your mother and I are going to get dinner ready. You two should get to know each other since you're going to be spending a lot of time together."

And then my parents both just left the room. And I was standing there, and he was standing there, and we were both just speechless. The silence was killing me.

"You were at the market, right? Were you watching me?"

"I wasn't watching you, I was just looking around at my new home."

Shoot, that's so embarrassing.

"Why are you here? I mean, why are you here alone? What made you come here?"

"Wow, you ask a lot of questions. I like your name. It's my favorite color. I hate when people say, my favorite color is green, or blue. That's so vague. I feel like if everyone is so unique, they should at least be able to find a shade of a color he or she likes the most, instead of something that millions of other people share. So, I don't like green, I like jade. What's your favorite color?"

He didn't answer my questions. But he complimented me. And he told me his favorite color. Which is one step closer to getting to know him. And he asked me what my favorite color is. He wants to get to know me! This is actually pretty awesome, now that I think about it. I'm always complaining how I don't have friends, and one literally shows up to my house to live with me.

"Probably ruby. It's so strong. There's no question in ruby; there's no doubt. Have you spoken to the hadas yet?"

"Uh, no. My situation is kind of complicated, as you can tell, since I'm living here, and I'm alone. I'm basically coming into this as part of your family. I don't really need an introduction with the hadas when I have a home, and I know more about this place then you'd think."

"Where are you from? How do you know about it here?"

"I'm from America. And I've done my research. But I've still got more to learn. I was kind of hoping you could be my own hada. What do you do all day if you're not in school?"

"Dinner's ready! Come on in the kitchen."

Sometimes parents can come in at the worse times. But maybe we needed the interruption. I could tell Storm about my walks in the park, but he might think it's weird that I'm so enthusiastic about a crystal. I could tell him that I help my parents around, but that would probably entail talking about how they're always teaching, and never really focusing on me. Definitely too personal for our first time meeting. And I certainly could not talk about how I spend countless hours thinking about the mystery man, and different scenarios of that man's life, and where he went after his conference with the hadas. So, I don't really know how to answer his question. But it seemed like he didn't know how to answer mine. I've got some investigating to do.

Chapter 5

I haven't been sleeping well lately. It's not because my phone is ringing off the hook, even though you'd think after days of ignoring them, these people would leave me alone. And it's not because Colby kissed me on the cheek, or wants to be hanging out with me 24/7, it's why he wants to be hanging out with me. Colby's got this great family to fall back on, so he can't even begin to understand why I might be hesitant in finding my mom. We've been sitting in my room for the past few hours, and I wish we were talking about something else, but this is his new obsession.

"Lily, I know this is sensitive and everything, but if you're upset that your mom isn't in your life, then wouldn't it make sense that you wanted to find her? Why aren't you jumping up and down at the chance?"

Maybe he's right; maybe I should be so excited to finally find her. I'm old enough now, where I guess it's possible. But this just wasn't the way I wanted it to happen. I've always dreamed she would just come back for my 18th birthday. She'd remember the day and everything. She run in and I'd be excited but I'd show her I was upset she'd been gone. She'd give me a really long heartfelt apology and after a while, I'd forgive her. She'd tell my dad she'd always been in love with him, and have a really awesome excuse for not being here for so long. Something like, she's in the CIA and was working a very difficult case, or she was being blackmailed by an ex-boyfriend who was holding her hostage and said he would kill her and all of us if she didn't stay with him.

"Lily, please let me in. I know you've got a hundred things running through your head right now, and I know its my fault, and I also know I should stop prying, but I'm your best friend and I want to be here for you. Don't you think we could have fun being detectives? I could be Bosley and you could be all three of

Charlie's Angels since your cooler
then all of them combined."

    And with that, he blushed, and
smiled. He looked up into my eyes
and didn't look away. He's so strong,
he can say anything he wants and
never look back.

"Its kind of complicated Colby. How
do you think we're even going to
begin to search for this woman?
She's such a mystery."

"Well, the apple clearly doesn't fall
far from the tree. So lets look at the
apple."

"Am I the apple?"

"It's looking like it considering she
is the tree."

"But that's not fair. I knew her for
such a short time, I'm probably
nothing like her. I don't think I'm
going to get us anywhere."

"Then it looks like we're going to
have to have a little chat with the
apple's dad."

"You can do that alone. I don't think daddy apple likes to talk about the tree. In fact, I know daddy apple doesn't like it, because I've been facing that fact for 16 years."

"But you're such a cute little apple, how can he resist?"

Whoa. Major flirt points for Colby right now. Is this because he's excited about the mystery, or he's just excited about me? Why is everything in my life so confusing? But, I can't get distracted. I knew sooner or later my dad and I were going to have this talk, but I guess it always seemed so distant. Now that it's real, it's getting scary. What do I ask? Where should I start? It's my summer before junior year, shouldn't I just be relaxing, not dealing with this? Then again, it's not like I'll be able to do it during the school year.

"Alright, Mr. Detective, we'll do it your way. But you better start making up a list of questions. You know how I get in awkward situations."

"Okay, but here's the thing. I think you may have to do it alone. If your dad didn't want to talk about it with you before, do you really think he'd want to talk about it with me? Sure, it's not like we're strangers and he knows this conversation is coming, but I don't think he's planning on me being there."

"But I need you. You're my rock, Bosley. You're the commander."

When I said that, he grabbed my hand. Every touch is electrifying. It's so hard focusing on finding my long lost mother when the boy I think I'm in love with is my sidekick.

"Lily, I'll be right here. I'll be waiting by the phone. I'll prep you for the conversation. You will never be alone, we're partners in crime remember?"

Okay, I know that finding my mom is a HUGE deal. It's life changing for me. And I know having this conversation with my dad will also be both of those. But how can I refuse Colby?

"Bosley, stop staring at me and start figuring out what I'm going to ask."

"YES! Lily, you're the best. Seriously, you are one of the strongest people I know."

"Yeah, yeah, yeah. Keep your eye on the prize buddy."

But I don't really want him to keep his eye on the prize. I want him to keep his eye on me. I want him to kiss me, to want to be with me, instead of wanting me to be having this conversation with my dad.

"Okay, well let's start off with the basics here. What do you know about her?"

Hmmm. What do I know? Honestly, I don't really know anything. I know her name was Ariella. I know she looked like me, because my dad always says that when he's feeling sentimental, or we're having a serious conversation.

I also know that somehow, she had the book. It's weird to think my mom had the one piece of evidence leading to this huge mystery of the Lost Land. How the heck did she get her hands on this?

"Her name is Ariella, and I'm told we look alike."

I feel stupid. How could that be all I know about her. She's my MOM. She gave birth to me, she named me, and I wouldn't be here without her, yet all I know is her name. Colby's going to think I'm so weird.

"Then this gives us a good icebreaker. You could start off with, how did you guys meet? Then follow it by, where is she from? It's almost a good thing you don't know that much, because then I'd be worried with all of the information you, had you still couldn't find her. We're beginning from square one, which means we've got a fresh start on the searching process. With information like where she was from, what she liked to do, and how they met, you can learn so much about her! Lily, we'll be with her in no time!"

Colby is pretty much the definition of perfection. Instead of making me feel bad about not knowing anything about my mom, he's being positive. He's so optimistic it's inspiring. I just wish I agreed with him.

"Why don't you talk to your dad tomorrow? We'll spend the rest of the day making sure you're comfortable with all of this, and figuring out what approach we're going to take for this conversation."

"Sounds good. Thanks, Colby, it really does mean a lot."

I'm seriously so thankful for Colby. Not only is he so enthusiastic about finding my mom, and helping me, but he never pushes too far. He wants me to be comfortable first, before he makes me do anything. And if it weren't for him, I'd never have the courage to talk to my dad, or try and find my mom at all. Still, I'm not sure I have what it takes to

have this conversation tomorrow.
This is going to be a long night.

Chapter 6

Dear Revista,

So Storm is amazing. He's funny, and kind, and extremely good-looking. The crystal is magenta today, the color of love. Is it too early to think that that may be a sign? Dinner last night was great. I still don't really know anything about him, but I think it's keeping me more intrigued.

Today's our first day together. My parents will be busy, as always, so he wants me to show him around. I'm kind of excited. The hadas are always visiting our house, and I know they're mystical creatures, but I still look to them with fascination. Now, he considers me a hada, and I have no problem with that! But if I'm going to be his hada, I need to know why it's now my role, and why he can't just meet with the real hadas.

"So, Storm, where do you want to go first?"

"I don't know, you tell me!"

"Let's just do an all around tour, and see where that leads us."

First, we went to Charriet's Fountain. Charriet's is where all of the tourists go when they first get here. It's a really large fountain, carved early on by some of the first people on the island. In the center is a statue of a girl named Charriet who was the wife of the artist behind it. He made her to look so beautiful, which is weird, because she's just a statue, but he must have really loved her because when you see it, it's kind of indescribable. It's like you know her and you're jealous of her elegance, but you also want to be her friend. Beneath the statue is a pale blue moat of flowing water. It mostly sits in the sun, but tourists like to jump in it. If you throw a coin in, you're supposed to get 9 years of good luck. It may just be a myth, but my dad said before he visited Charriet's, he hadn't met my mom, and he hadn't had me.

"Do you want to throw a coin in? It's supposed to bring you good luck for 9 years."

"Do I look like I need luck? I'm with a beautiful girl on a beautiful island. But, this fountain is really nice, do you come here a lot?"

HE CALLED ME BEAUTIFUL! I have to keep calm.

"Not really. At some point, it just became another place I walk through."

We stayed at Charriet's for a while. We watched all of the tourists come in and out, and made up fake back-stories on them. There was a tall skinny girl we named Angela because her head was up so high we wouldn't be able to tell if she had a halo on or not. Storm said that she had come down from Heaven because she needed a vacation, and since the island is the most beautiful place to go, she came here. All of the angels come here, we just happened to only see Angela. Then there was a rather large, tan man with sweat

*beading down his forehead and his
muscular back. The weirdest part
about him was that he wasn't bad
looking, so we called him Fabio. He
was with his girlfriend, a tiny girl,
equally as tan as him, but almost half
of the size. She had dark defined eyes
that were lined thickly with black.
Her hair was up in a bun and she
seemed completely content. We
decided it was because Fabio kept
her so safe, being as strong as he
was. We named her Georgina
because her bathing suit was the
color of peaches, and Storm said in
America there's a place called
Georgia that's famous for having
peaches.*

*There was also a young boy
bouncing around the fountain, and
he seemed to be alone. We named
him Rabbit because he jumped up
down a lot. I joked that he was like
Storm, no family in sight. Storm
looked intensely at the boy like he
was waiting for something. From
across the fountain we heard a man
shouting for his son, whose real
name was Michael. Storm's stiff
shoulders relaxed as the boy ran into*

his father's arms and we both decided we like the name Rabbit better than Michael. Storm wanted to go tell the boy that he should self-proclaim himself Rabbit instead, but I wouldn't let him because his dad didn't seem that happy and Michael started to wander again.

Why is it so easy for Storm to create a story about these strangers' lives, but he can't tell me his own? At some point, I'm going to find out. He's living with me and we'll be spending every day together, so I can be patient. I know it's not long before he trusts me enough. When we were leaving Charriet's, I saw Storm pull out a coin from his pocket and toss it in the fountain. I guess he didn't want me to see, so I pretended like I was focused on our next destination. What kind of luck is he looking for?

"Do most people who live here, live here all of their lives?"

"Yeah. It's kind of like an everlasting cycle. You're born here, you grow up here, you have kids

here, and you die here. The lists of generations for some of these people are crazy!"

"Yeah, I guess I get that. Why would anyone want to leave? It's beautiful, and dreaming is probably so much easier then making money."

"I don't know, people can still get bored. If you lived somewhere all of your life, wouldn't you want to see if there's anything out there for you?"

"Not if something is keeping you where you are."

Why is Storm asking me all of these questions, but not answering any of mine? This whole discovery is a lot harder then I thought. He said if something was keeping you where you were, you'd stay. It seems to me he had a reason to be in America. So why is he here? Maybe what was keeping him there isn't keeping him anymore.

"What's it like, making money?" I asked.

"It's time consuming. And a pain in general. Some people live awful lives because they can't make enough. I'm lucky I've never had to experience that, but I've seen some terrible things."

"If your life at home was so great, why did you leave?"

"If your life here is so great, why do you want to leave?"

"I never said I wanted to leave."

"Jade, please. You're good looking, smart, and curious, but you are not hard to read. I saw the way you took offense when I questioned why anyone would want to get away from here. I wasn't trying to upset you, I'm just trying to find out more about my new home."

"Well, I'm trying to find out more about you. You're good looking, smart, and curious, AND you're hard to read. Storm, we're about to be spending every single day together, you're going to need to open up."

"Wow, what is this?"

How convenient. We happened to arrive at La Playa de Greel. La Playa de Greel is one of the best beaches on the island, at least in my opinion. It has velvety soft sand that's a mix between white and golden. The water defines the meaning of the color turquoise, and it's clearer than a piece of glass. The weather varies between gorgeous sunny skies to soothing thunderstorms. Thunderstorms on a beach seem off-putting, but until you've experienced it at La Playa de Greel, you can't even begin to imagine what it's like. It's the most peaceful and amazing thing, like finally something on this island understands that life isn't always a ball of sunshine and perfection. La Playa de Greel is a little tortured, and I love it.

"It's called La Playa de Greel. It's one of the beaches by our house. Some people think this is the prettiest beach in all of País de los Sueños, but for me it's more then that."

"Why?"

"If I answer will you answer one of my questions?"

He nodded.

"When I was little, my parents used to make every Sunday "Jade Day". They'd have to teach every other day, but they made sure they were free Sunday's so we could hang out. I always got to pick where I wanted to go, it could have been anywhere on the island, but I kept coming back here. Here is where I felt the closest with them, it was stress-free and a good time. We'd swim in the ocean with all of the animals and explore new places every time. Even though it was the same place, there was always something new. New fish to see, a new reef to dive down to. Here is where I met my first mermaid."

"Mermaids? No way. This place just gets better and better. Can I meet a mermaid?"

"Probably, if you're here for long enough. There are things that only locals get to see, and mermaids are one of them. They're pretty rare, and I don't think they want a lot of people to know about them, so it takes a while before they'll reveal themselves to you. But trust me, if you swim in this water they'll be there too. They're extremely curious so they're always watching; you just can't notice them because they're really cunning. They're usually pretty deep or hidden behind something so it's never apparent that they're there, but they are. They're really nice too, and a blast to swim with because they know the ocean better then you can even imagine. If you actually end up talking to them, I guarantee you your life will change."

"Can't you just take me in? I really want to meet one. If they know you, they'll come out, right?"

"Not necessarily. It's the first time I'd be bringing you, they don't even know if I trust you. Give it time, Storm, you'll get there some day."

"Will you tell me about one then?"

"Sure. I met one named Drake when I was eight. His mother was very sick, so he was out looking for certain plants to heal her. I kind of bumped into him, and I thought he'd be really freaked out, because he didn't know if he could trust me, but instead he said, 'Hey Jade. Nice to finally meet you.' Which was crazy because I'd never seen him before or heard of him. He saw that I was confused and explained to me that he was dating one of my friends Leeza. Leeza was the first mermaid that I'd ever met, but apparently she told all of her friends about me, so they'd know to trust me to. It explained a lot, Drake was really handsome and Leeza was beautiful. Both had chestnut brown hair but Drake had light purple eyes and Leeza had deep pink eyes. Oh yeah, mermaids have all kinds of colored eyes. Pretty much any color you can imagine, except white and black I think. Drake told me that him and Leeza were actually going to get married soon, and he seriously needed to find

medicine for his mom so she could make it to the wedding. It was her dying wish."

Storm's eyes were teary.

"Did she make it?"

"Yeah! I told Drake I'd help him look, but I didn't know the ocean like he did, so I kind of just accompanied him while he looked. If you're friendly with a mermaid, they'll give you a jewel attached to a shell string that you wear tightly around your head, and it makes you able to breathe underwater. Even then, though, I couldn't swim as deep as him, so I was really just someone he could talk to while he was distressed. He told me all about how much he loved Leeza, he said his love for her was bigger then the ocean, her beauty was more powerful than a cyclone, and he'd do just about anything for her. Drake was one of the most passionate and kindhearted mermaids I'd ever met, though honestly, they're all really nice. Why would you be mean when you're a mermaid? Life is amazing."

"But there are still problems, Jade. Just like how I can't understand why you'd want to leave here. Nothing's perfect."

"I guess that's true."

"So, do you have any of the jewels that let you breathe underwater? Could we try them?"

"No! You don't keep them, silly. It's dangerous in the water. Mermaids know how to maneuver, to fight sharks or whales or squids, if they need. Humans do not. It's not safe unless you're with a mermaid. I wouldn't want to be alone anyways."

"Yeah, I get that. So, do you still come here every Sunday with your parents?"

"No, not at all. When I turned ten, the island started to get more populated, and my parents were forced to start working on Sunday. I kept trying to come back, but it wasn't the same. Every time I'm here, I wish I could go back in time,

*back when I'd run onto the velvet
sand and be free from my life."*

*He got really quiet. Maybe
opening up like that was too early.
He probably thinks I'm weird now,
that I'm still dying for the affection
of mommy and daddy.*

*"But, this is probably just a beach to
you—"*

*"Jade, thank you for sharing that
with me. I've had family problems
too, and I can see in your eyes how
sacred this place is for you."*

*"Yeah, okay. You're just trying to
distract me so I don't remember that
I get to ask you a question now. So
here it is: why are you here, and
where is your family?"*

*"First of all, that's two questions,
you get one. Second, I'm not trying
to distract you. I really do want to
get to know you."*

*"Well, then thanks. But I don't
believe it. And fine, my question is
why are you here?"*

"Why are you incapable of believing that you're worth something? You put everyone before you Jade, and you've got to start doing something for yourself. And I'm here, because this is where you've lead me on our tour."

How does he do that? I've known him for like 48 hours and he can already tell anyone everything about me. I wish I could say the same for him, but I really have no idea who he is.

"No way Storm. You're not getting away with that answer. I meant why are in País de los Sueños?"

"One question Jade. You had only one."

"Are you seriously going to be like this? You know so much about me, it's not fair."

"Fine. Just because I don't like to see my new friend upset. I'm here because one of my family members passed away, someone who I was

very close with. They left a letter for me, explaining a lot that I didn't know about them. They asked me to come here, so, here I am."

"Something you didn't know about them? I'm finding that hard to believe. You seem to be pretty good at understanding people."

"Jade, there's a lot you don't know about me."

"Storm, trust me, you don't have to say that twice."

Chapter 7

Sylvia and I hung out today, which was good because she is pretty much my only friend other than Colby, but the whole time I was thinking about this conversation with my dad. We're really not that close, definitely not close enough to talk about it. It was silly to think that hanging out with her could distract me. She kept looking at me and saying,

"Lil, what's going on? Something's obviously up."

"Nah, it's nothing."

We're friends but not close enough for me to spill my life story like that. Colby was the only one I really trusted.

"If it's nothing, then is it okay if I ask you something?"

"Yeah, whatever you want. But if it's about the book, I'm not answering."

"It's not about the book. It's about Colby. Do you know who he's interested in?"

"No, we don't really talk about that stuff, why?"

"It's funny, you guys seem like best friends, I thought for sure you'd know. I was just wondering. I mean, he's kind of irresistible. He's amazing looking and he's really nice."

"Yeah, he's awesome."

"If I were to tell you that someone liked him, would you be able to help me out?"

"Well I'm sure that a ton of people like him, but who is it?"

I didn't agree because why would I? No way do I want to set Colby up with someone unless it's me.

"Can I trust you?"

"Sylvia, come on. Who am I going to tell?"

"Just don't tell Colby. But, it's me. I really like him. We have math class together and he always knows what to say. I get kind of nervous, but he doesn't let me be uncomfortable around him. I love that about him. I'm sure you know what I'm talking about, but I was hoping that he'd see me as more then a friend."

What is that supposed to mean? That I know what she's saying only she wants to be more than his friend? I could be more then his friend too. Either way, this is nothing I want to deal with. Sylvia is pretty much my only friend, and I don't want to upset her, but does this really have to happen? I'm having a hard enough time trying to get Colby on my side, and I need to deal with my dad, which reminds me.

"Uh, sure Sylvia. I'll talk to him, but casually so he doesn't know, don't worry. I have to go, though, I have this thing with my dad. It's kind of important."

"Ah, Lily you're the best! The other girls clearly don't understand how nice you are. They all said you'd want Colby for yourself, but I knew you guys were just friends. I'll see you later!"

I left, livid. What other girls? Why were they talking about me? I don't know them. And the sad part is, the other girls were right. But why did Sylvia just assume that Colby and I were just friends? She doesn't know what goes on between us, she barely even knows me. Pretty much the only things she knows is that I moved a lot and Colby and I are really good friends. I would begin to question her motives of being friends with me, but I've got way more to worry about as I walk in my door.

I don't think I've ever been as nervous as I am now. Going to a new school and making a whole new set of friends each year? That's a piece of cake compared to what I'm about to do. I have to though, it's what Colby wants, and I think it's what I want. I do want to find my mom, and this is the only way I'm going to, so I need to face my fears. My dad's in the kitchen, reading the newspaper. I think it's now or never because he's always in a good mood when he just gets to relax and read the paper.

"Dad, can I ask you something?"

"Sure, Lil."

"Well, it might be something you don't want to answer. Like, about someone you don't like to talk about."

He looks up from the paper, and just stares at me. Then he sighs.

"Here goes the mother conversation right? And you won't be happy if I just tell you we were in love and you look like her and you're turning into someone that she would be proud of?"

"No, Dad. I was wondering where she's from. I feel like its time for me to learn about her. We don't have to talk about it again, but I'm sixteen and I think it's only fair for me to know."

"Oh, sweetie, you're right. I guess it's just hard to talk about. I should have had this conversation a long time ago, but I'm not as strong as you."

"Dad, please. You're the strongest man I know, you were the one that had to deal with her leaving, I was so small I'm sure I didn't even realize."

"Ha! Didn't realize? You realized all right. You used to cry every day. No matter how much I held you, and tried to comfort you, you kept crying. I knew her leaving would be a missing piece to your puzzle for the rest of your life, but I didn't realize it would hit you that quickly. And it broke my heart."

I don't say anything. I've never heard him say anything like that, and it kills me to see how bad my mom hurt my dad. Maybe I don't want to find her.

"But we met in college. She was from another country, but she came to America for school. I was a cool kid in college, though you may find it hard to believe, and I was never lonely when it came to the ladies. But sophomore year, I went to a party, and I noticed this painstakingly beautiful woman in the corner of the room. She was laughing with another guy, and immediately I wanted to punch him in the face and push him away. That's when I knew I liked her. I went up to the guy and politely whispered in his ear that if he didn't get his hands off of my girlfriend I'd rip him to shreds. You should've seen his face. He ran immediately which was crazy to me because as threatening as I made myself seem, how could you run from a girl like that? We ended up talking the whole night and I had already felt my entire world change the minute I looked into her glowing eyes. I had never felt that way before about a girl, usually they came to me, and I didn't have many emotions towards them. But she was different. She had long dark brown hair and a smile that could warm your heart. She was always smiling too, which made it hard, because everywhere we went, everyone wanted to know her, including some very good looking guys. She was friendly towards everyone, but she told me I was the one she wanted to be with when I got jealous. She wasn't the type of girl to leave, even if she knew there was someone out there that was better then me."

He said she wasn't the type of girl to leave. He realized right after saying that he'd made a mistake, but it just got really quiet, and he looked at me. I felt like I needed to break the silence.

"So, then, when she left, it wasn't for someone else?"

"No, sweetie! It wasn't. She had things she had to deal with back home. I never met her family, but they had an important role where she lived, and she needed to go back to make sure everything was in order. Her mom died when she was younger, and her dad was getting sick. She went back to be with him. I guess I thought that when her father passed away, she'd come back to us. I wouldn't have let her go if I knew how this would turn out."

"Dad, you can't blame it on yourself. Mom was going to do what she was going to do. Did she ever write, or call?"

"I wish I could say she did. I really have no idea what's happened to her Lil. If I did, I'd tell you everything."

"Well, that's okay, Dad. What did her family do that was so important?"

"I don't know. She never told me. I always figured they were like, royalty, or something. I don't even know exactly where she was from. She told me the name of it once, but she never said it again. She always said she just didn't want to talk about it. And when I was with her, I couldn't think of anything else, but how beautiful she was, and how much I wanted to be with her forever. I guess I was too distracted to ask questions. Then when she got pregnant, I was really distracted! I started freaking out about how I was going to support us! We were just out of college, and I was so inexperienced. Luckily, I landed a small job at my company now, and it turned into something that could support us for the rest of our lives, but that was very stressful. We had to buy a house, buy baby things, take classes on being parents, and prepare ourselves mentally. The ironic thing is, the only way I remained calm was I kept reminding myself that this amazing woman that I was in love with was going to be taking care of my child. In my eyes, your mother was unstoppable. Sure, she was wild at heart, but she was determined. She was super girl to me, and I knew nothing could faze her. The only time I saw her break down was when she told me she was leaving."

"So, she didn't want to go?"

"No! Not in the slightest. She was the strongest woman I have ever known, but that day, she was like a fragile, innocent, child. She cried and cried and kept saying if she didn't go bad things were going to come. She needed to go back. I like to think of her as more of a hero, rather then someone who abandoned us. I remember the day she told me like it was yesterday. I always replay it, wondering if there is something I could have changed."

"What happened?"

"We took you on a walk by the beach. Your mother loved the beach, and said that she wanted you to love it too, so we used to go there a lot. I'd always sit on a towel while you guys would laugh and play in the water. But this time, there was a brisk, sea breeze, and the beach was pretty much empty. You were asleep in my arms, and Ariella said, 'I've got something to tell you. I can't have you make this harder then it is, and trust me, this is very hard.' And then she started crying. I'd never seen her cry before. I stopped walking and sat there silently. I knew whatever was coming was going to change my life, because Ariella was never serious like that, and she

never, ever, shed a tear, at least not
in my presence. She told me she got
a message from a friend from home,
and that her father was sick. She
needed to be back to take care of her
father, and make sure that everything
was still in order. I asked her what
she was talking about, what she
needed to check on, but she wouldn't
answer. She said she didn't want to
leave, but she kept saying, 'I have to.
It's only right. I have to. It's only
right.' I had a feeling she wasn't just
talking about seeing her father before
he passed away. We walked home
silently; I couldn't begin to conjure
up words in response. Her tears
continued to fall lightly, like when
the rain just begins to drizzle. She
was even beautiful when she cried. I
didn't have anything to say, maybe
because I was so shocked, maybe
because I felt betrayed. My whole
world, or what it had become, was
being flipped upside down. All I
could say is, 'Are you taking Ryan?'
but that made her cry more. Finally,
she spit out that she couldn't take
you because she was from a
dangerous place. She thought you'd
be safer here with me. The next

morning I begged and pleaded that she let us come with her. Your mother was worth the danger to me, and I knew I could protect you. I would do anything for the two women in my life. But all she did was cry. She wouldn't let us come with her, and she wouldn't stay."

Then he started to cry. I hugged him and he said:

"I waited for eight years, hoping for a call, a letter, an email, but they never came. Every year on your birthday I ran to the post office thinking she'd send you something. She may have forgotten about me but she loved you like I've never seen love before. I was in love with your mother, crazily in love, and she was in love with me, but boy did she love you. I never heard from her again, and I've looked. I just can't find her."

"Well, what if I gave it a try? What if I looked for her?"

"Lily, you are so adorable for caring like this, but I've tried. Trust me, it's hopeless."

"Dad, adorable, really? Don't call me adorable for caring. I think I can find her. I mean did you try your hardest? Maybe I could try harder."

"Lily, I would do anything to get your mother back. Don't insult me."

"How about YOU don't insult ME. Have some faith Dad. She's my mom! I have a fresh set of eyes and a different perspective. And I've got a friend who wants to help me."

"Lily, I knew your mother better then anybody else in this world. Don't you think I searched all of the obvious places? And, I'm sorry, you and Colby may be a great pair, but that doesn't mean your going to find your mom."

"So you looked everywhere Dad? Are you sure? Did you look at the Lost Land?"

"Lily, don't be ridiculous. No one knows where the Lost Land is, and why in the world would your mother be there?"

"Clearly, you don't know her as well as you think dad. The only thing that's ridiculous is your lack of faith in your daughter."

He doesn't know about the book.

Chapter 8

Dear Revista,

I can't stop thinking about what Storm said to me yesterday, about his family members. I'm obsessing over this small detail because it's all I know about him, and I guess I'm just so anxious to know more. We stayed at La Playa de Greel for a really long time yesterday, so long that it started to thunder and we had to leave. He decided that I have to take him to the La Playa de Greel every morning before we start our day, that way the mermaids will eventually talk to him. We're going to finish the tour after that, and it seems like he's more open to talking when we're alone like that, so I'm pretty excited.

I also can't stop thinking about how he makes me feel. After we each shared our personal moments, we didn't talk much, but it wasn't really weird. We just sat and watched the wave's lights kiss the shoreline, then retreat back. We sat on the warm sand and I ran my hands through it over and over as I watched Storm take in his surroundings. He was using his senses to develop an interpretation about the place; he was hearing laughter, smelling the salty ocean breeze, seeing the sun sparkling on the ocean, touching the soft sand, and tasting the freedom the beach gave off.

Then we watched the people around us. There were plenty of happy families who were once as carefree as I was, and I was content with watching them. Storm knew it; I could tell by the way he was studying my face, and my emotions. I pretended like I didn't see, because even though I find it annoying that he knows WAY more about me then I do for him, I like that he cares. I feel so comfortable with him, because it feels like I've got nothing to hide. Maybe I shouldn't let my guard down so much, especially since he's such a mystery to me. Why should I be okay with the way we are? Well, I'm not okay with it, but right now it's not a choice. I guess I just have to keep that in mind, so I don't

*embarrass myself, or do something
stupid. I need to know I can trust him
before I completely relax.*

*When Storm comes into the
room, freshly showered after our
swim and ready for the tour, part
two, I can't help but get weak in the
knees. The way his hair glistens
when it is wet, and how the dark
shading makes his light eyes pop. We
start down the trail past Charriet's
and La Playa de Greel and turn into
Casara's Court.*

*Casara's is a beautifully
landscaped garden that was once the
prized possession of a Queen named
Queen Margareta Casara. She was
widowed but she had many friends.
When her friends went back to their
husbands and wives, she took up the
hobby of gardening. She traveled all
over to find the world's most
beautiful flowers to fill her garden
with, and the outcome was
outstanding. It's home to lush
purples, dainty pinks, light yellows,
vibrant reds, and strong oranges.
Each flower is delicate to the touch,
as soft as a kiss, and yet the flowers*

show the Queen's strength through the tough loss of her beloved husband Daniel, who loved her so dearly. Daniel and Margareta had a tough relationship, but no matter what they'd always come back to each other because of the strength of their love.

Queen Margareta was devastated by the loss of her husband, and the only thing that kept her going was her garden. She said every time she visited she'd see Daniel, for both her flowers and her husband had everlasting beauty, so even though Daniel wasn't there, his presence was infinite. She died of old age, at one hundred and one years old, and was buried beneath one of the flower beds. Every once in a while someone will come and trim and water the plants, but they withstand storms and droughts all by themselves. Some say it's a miracle, but I know nothing is more powerful than the strength of a determined, persistent, young woman.

"You can touch one of the flowers if you want, Storm. Trust me, you're not going to hurt it."

"Are you sure? They're so precious. I wouldn't want to do anything wrong."

"I'm positive."

When he touched the pink cypress vine, one of the Queen's favorite flowers, his whole body softened.

"It's so lovely. Like nothing I've ever felt before."

"You don't have these in America?"

"Nope. We have sunflowers, and daises, and if you want to be romantic, you can buy roses from a shop. But nothing like this."

"I'd love to see the sunflowers. I've heard of them, how they're tall and fragile, and are brightly colored. I'd love to see them in person."

"Jade, why is it you want to go to America so badly? Look at these flowers, to you, they're just another piece of Casara, but to me, they're amazing. I've never seen anything like what I've seen here, America is plain; País de los Sueños is fascinating."

"Storm, you think you know it all. I understand we offer beautiful things here, but that's not everything. Most of these people will die only knowing what they've seen here. If you didn't travel, you wouldn't be able to see País de los Sueños. I believe you can never truly understand someone, until you've walked on their soil, and seen the land they've seen."

"I agree with you, you do have to walk in a man's footsteps to understand where he's coming from. That's what my father wanted me to do. That's what I'm doing."

"Wait what? Your father?

He stopped from looking at the flowers and stared up at me. He looked sad, and there was a story in his eyes. A long one, nothing short of complicated.

"I told you a family member had passed away. My father wrote in his letter he wanted me to come here, to walk in his footsteps and solve something he'd lived with his whole life."

"Solve what? Your father was here? In País de los Sueños? Maybe my parents knew him! Someone here has to know him, it's a pretty tight community."

"No, Jade, this is not something we're going to be asking around about. He wasn't here long, I'm sure no one knows him, so drop it."

"Why are you being so weird about it? I thought you were close. Don't you miss him? Maybe if I ask around, you'll be able to solve whatever it is your father asked of you."

"NO. Jade, please, leave it alone."

I wanted so badly to ask around, because I knew someone could lead me to something, something more than what Storm already knew. But I wanted Storm to trust me. I didn't want him to stop opening up just because he thought I could potentially ruin something he'd shared with me.

"Fine, whatever. But I feel like if I'm going to be keeping a secret, I'd like to know more about it, just in case. What's the deal with the mystery you're solving?"

"It's a mystery Jade, obviously if I knew more I wouldn't be here."

"Well, what do you know so far?"

"I know my father came here, but he didn't stay long. He said he wasn't exactly welcome—"

"That's ridiculous, everyone is welcome here."

"Are you going to interrupt me, or let me tell you what I know?"

"I know that he was forced to leave. My dad believes something is wrong here, and he wants me to investigate. We were a lot alike, but my dad said that the one thing I had that he didn't was courage. He knew I'd be able to see the problems he was seeing, but he thought I could stop them, instead of running away, like him."

"Wow. You must've really been close. I love it here, and if there's a problem, I want to help. I'm not exactly the courageous type, but it seems like you can play that role for both of us."

I expected Storm to smile when I said this. He always kind of smiled when I was done talking. But he didn't smile. He just asked me where the next place was. I guess he was done looking at Casara's.

"Next is Estrella's Cliff."

"Estrella? That's Spanish for star, I know that one!"

"Yeah, and that's pretty much a big part of it. Ancient legend says there

*was a girl named Estrella who loved
a man name Luneius. He was kind
and beautiful but he was cursed. His
curse was that he was forced to help
anyone and everyone that needed
him; he was unable to refuse. This
seems like a nice thing, and couldn't
harm him, but it did. The evil witch
who cursed him was also in love with
him. Luneius and Estrella were mad
for each other and when the witch
saw him look at Estrella the way he
did, she knew she needed to interrupt
their love. She pretended to be
Estrella's friend and called her over
for dinner one night. Meanwhile, on
the same night, she asked Luneius
for help. She needed him to fix a
creak in her door at her house. While
he was over, Estrella started to walk
through the door for dinner, and the
witch begged Luneius to kiss her,
saying she needed his help to feel
loved. Though Luneius loved Estrella
with all of his heart, he could not
refuse the witch, and Estrella walked
in just in time to see the two kissing.
She could not believe her eyes and
ran away. Everywhere she went
reminded her of Luneius and their
love, so she continued to run until*

*she could get away. He ran after her,
but he wasn't quick enough. She got
to the peak of the cliff and knew
there was nowhere else to go but up,
so she jumped into the sky, and like
her heart, she shattered into pieces.
What you know as stars are actually
pieces of Estrella and the super shiny
ones are her tears. Luneius arrived
heart broken and jumped up to be
with her. When he got to the sky she
was already scattered everywhere
and he tried to put the pieces back
together. When you see a crescent
moon with two sides peeking out,
that's Luneius reaching for his
love."*

*"Wow, that's crazy. Do you actually
believe that?"*

*"Well, I mean, it's a myth, but yeah,
why not? What other reason do you
have for why the stars are the way
they are, and the moon shaped the
way it is?"*

*"No, I mean, do you believe a love
like that? A love so strong they both
ended their lives and ended up being
eternally and tragically frozen."*

"It's not so tragic, think about how many romances bloom over the beauty of the stars. Taking someone to see the shiny stars at night is pretty much the most romantic thing you can do."

"Oh yeah? And we just happen to be hitting the cliff as the sun sets?"

It wasn't exactly on purpose, but it was true. As we got to Estrella's the sun started to set. It's the most beautiful spot on the island to be at, especially with the sun setting. I decided instead of making the moment awkward, I'd have fun with it. Dad and I always used to come and jump off the cliffs here; they're not that high and the ocean below is really deep. It was always so exhilarating, and if Storm had the adventure in him that I thought he did, I knew he'd be down to have fun.

"Oh Storm, what do you mean? You're making me uncomfortable with this talk! So uncomfortable I may just have to jump!"

I ripped off my clothes until I was only in my bathing suit, if you live on an island like this you're always prepared to swim, and ran towards the edge. As I was running I heard,

"Jade, No! I was kidding! Don't go all Estrella on me! C'mon!"

Hitting the water after a jump from Estrella's is one of the most refreshing things. You're flying in the air, then immersed in beautiful, crystal clear, salty water. No stress here. Just like Estrella, the jump is meant to get away from it all. I came up laughing. I bobbed in the cool water as I noticed Storm timidly peer over the edge, afraid of what he might see.

"Jade! What the heck! You scared me!"

"Are you coming in or do I need to hold your hand while you jump?"

He laughed, ripped off his shirt, and plunged in. I'm still getting used to this sight. Storm has the body of a

Greek God. He's tan and has strong, chiseled shoulders that automatically scream, "I can and have fought off multiple monters who get in my way." His stomach is tight and muscled.

"That was awesome!"

"Right? Estrella knows her stuff!"

"It's like the most freeing thing I've ever done!"

Jumping off a cliff is pretty drastic; I can't imagine what he's done that's crazier.

"Really, and what's the most 'freeing thing you've ever done?'"

"This."

He said and kissed me. In the water. Under the stars at Estrella's Cliff. Storm kissed me. I don't think I could write it enough times to believe it. That was by far the most beautiful moment I have ever experienced. Screw the island I live on, and the crystal that shines for me every day,

I've got a beautiful boy who wants to kiss me under the stars as we float together in the ocean by a cliff. And not just kiss me, move me. That's what his kiss did, it changed me. It was delicate, but strong. It was everything I've ever wanted, but nothing I've known. I'll never be the same.

Chapter 9

Colby's pretty excited about everything I've found out about my mom. He's even more excited about the fact that my dad didn't know about the book. He thinks if we pool all of our resources together, my dad, the book, and me, then we can easily find her.

The problem is, my mind is on the fight I had with my dad. I didn't tell Colby that our conversation ended the way it did. Colby's family is perfect, his mom used to be a model but now she stays home and takes care of the kids. His dad is an anchor on the *Today Show* and practically a hero to the many Americans who watch it. His brother, Doug, is in college and he adores Colby, they used to play football and lacrosse together all of the time. Doug used to be really athletic but he's gotten more and more interested in history and geography. He's pretty much head over heels ecstatic that I have the journal leading to the Lost Land.

They're just such a close-knit family, and nothing that I can relate to. My dad and I barely speak, and when we tried to have a serious conversation, it ended horribly. I was hoping my dad could be a good reference to have when finding her— I mean he does know her really well–but it seems like Colby and I will be doing all of the investigating by ourselves.

"Lil, did your dad give you anything of hers that we can look at, something that can lead us to her?"

"No, all I have is the journal."

"Well, why don't we ask him if he has anything?"

"He doesn't, he told me."

So that wasn't completely the truth. But he did say she never called or wrote, so I'm going off of that. In fact the only thing I have from her is the lilac letter I found in the back of the book. I don't know if I'm ready to open it though and I know if I tell Colby I'd have no choice.

"It sucks we don't even know what country she is from. I mean, countries are big, but we're not even narrowed down to one."

"Yeah, but my dad said she loved the beach. She's probably from somewhere warm."

"Ooh, maybe she's from Australia, or Jamaica. That would be so cool. If we had to go fly out to find her, I'd be fine with that, just saying."

Money isn't exactly an object in Colby's life. With a famous dad, and a mom who used to be famous, he'd be happy to pay for both of us.

"Yeah, I'd be fine with that too, Colb."

"Well, what else did your dad say? I feel stumped honestly. There are so many places with beaches, the only clue we have is that she doesn't live in America, but she could be anywhere."

"The thing is, even if we find where she's from, we may still not find her. Sure, it'd be really helpful, but she went back home fifteen years ago. A lot can happen in fifteen years."

"Lily, don't think like that! I'm sure if she could've left, she would've come right back here to find you."

"Yeah, yeah, yeah. So, Colby, you wanted to find her so badly, what do we do next?"

"Hmm…"

I love the face he makes when he thinks. His nose gets scrunched up and his eyes glisten, like he's always got a million things running through his mind that are about to rock his world.

"Let's look at the book. I mean, your mom had it for a reason, and there might be a clue about her in it. Maybe Jade knew her. Did Jade or Storm ever say anything about an Ariella?"

"No, but Jade and Storm were also alive a long time ago. I'm sure they didn't know my mom."

"Ms. Negative, I may have to find a new partner in crime if this pessimistic act keeps up."

He laughed as I lead him to the book. Colby's read the book numerous times. After I told him about it, we spent the entire day reading it. Since then, he's never wanted to leave it alone.

"Lily, I need you in here," my dad calls.

"Alright, you know where it is, make yourself at home." I say to Colby as I head towards the kitchen.

What could my dad possibly want? I thought he wasn't speaking to me after yesterday. What if he bans Colby from coming over? Ugh, maybe I should just go back to my room.

"Lil, I've been thinking about yesterday. I'm really sorry I lashed out at you; it was out of line. You know I'm not completely strong when it comes to your mom, and I felt like you questioned how much I wanted her back."

"Dad, I would never. I know you love her and—"

"And I was wrong. I realize that maybe your mother isn't something that I'm ready to deal with yet, but Lily, you are. You're brave and you're just like her. I want you to have this."

He hands me a beautiful ring. It's got a simple gold band with clear diamond-like jewels surrounding a midsized ruby. It was my mother's, I can already tell, and when I slip it on, I feel her spirit moving through me.

"Dad, I don't know what to say."

"I do. Good luck on your search for your mother. I'm positive you'll find her."

I have the greatest father in the world. He didn't need to explain to me why he wasn't helping me. I understood then that he didn't feel emotionally ready to face the monstrous size of the mystery of my mom, but he believed I was. As we hugged, I realized that maybe my family wasn't Colby's, but I didn't need it to be. I was walking on stars as I headed back into my room, until I saw Colby sitting on my bed staring at the door waiting for me. With a lilac envelope in his hands.

"Lily, what is this?"

Chapter 10

Dear Revista,

Oh Revista! You'd think what I'd be writing today is nothing but lovesick puppy notes on how incredible Storm is. He really is amazing, Revista. He's been treating my like his girlfriend, like we've been together for years, and he makes me feel so comfortable. I don't know why, but I feel like I know him so well, like I trust him with my life. I could go on and on about him, and I would love to do that— but something horrible has happened and I just can't exactly get my thoughts together.

You see, the day started out really awesome. After last night I felt fearless. Since Storm and I ended up staying at Estrella's until the sun rose, we woke up late and I told him I wanted to finish the tour. He was more then happy to oblige, especially because we both knew if we were off touring the island we'd have time alone again. We started off at La

Playa de Greel, for our usual morning swim. It was only day two of Storm being in the water, and I still don't really believe it, but somehow the mermaids knew to trust him. I think it was because we were kissing in the water, and they know me well enough to feel my emotions and understand.

Storm was awestruck when Delia swam up and handed us each a jewel. Mine was a diamond, Storm's a ruby. He switched with me because he remembered that ruby was my favorite. Delia took us on a tour of her home and showed us where Drake and Leeza live, explaining to my surprise that they now had a child! It had been years since I'd been in the water, and I'd really missed a lot. I wanted so badly to meet the child but all three of them weren't home. Delia swims so gracefully you almost forget where you are and where you're going. She has bright red hair and deep green eyes that are so powerful it's hard to look straight into them. If it weren't for her long red hair, we definitely would have lost her. I was proud of

Storm, he played it cool around her and kept up with us. When it was all over and we were back on shore he started freaking out about how amazing it was, saying he practically peed his pants when she popped up next to us. I just laughed. How could I not? Then, we began the final chapter of our tour.

"So today we'll see the park, you're really going to love it. The park is my favorite place in the world, and I have something special to show you."

While walking to the park we went past the market. I grabbed Storm's hand and pushed through the crowd to get to Melinda. I wanted her to meet him. She was like a second mom to me and Storm was my first kiss so I had to have them meet. Of course, I didn't tell her that, but I thought it would be important. Melinda looked from Storm to me when we arrived and gave me a wink.

"Mel, this is Storm. He's my new friend here. I wanted you to meet him."

"Hi, Storm, how do you do?"

"I'm great, thanks! Jade tells me a lot about you."

"I hope all good things! After all, Jade is practically my daughter. We've spent countless hours chatting about our favorite crystal color, our hopes, our dreams, what's happening in our families. I'm sure she'll be coming back soon to tell me how amazing you are."

"Melinda, come on now."

Storm laughed and squeezed my shoulder. Melinda noticed and winked again.

"Listen guys, I'd love to talk but today is super busy and I've got to start dealing with all of these people. What can I say; people love bread! It was nice meeting you, Storm. Take good care of her."

"I will. Nice meeting you too!"

Great. I knew they'd get along, but it made me feel better. I was more comfortable kissing the boy who I knew my parents and my almost parent liked. But more importantly, I wanted to take Storm to the park.

I couldn't wait to see the look on Storm's face when he saw the crystal. He's adventurous and would be engulfed in its beauty, I just knew it. I wanted to see the color of the day reflecting off of his hazel eyes, and the way his chiseled cheekbones looked as he raised his head to see the large monument. Maybe, today would be light pink, and I could explain to him that this meant destiny. Destiny between two people, maybe. I wondered what he would say, about destiny. I wondered if he even considered the two of us meeting, destiny. Either way, I knew the crystal would rock him. I thought for sure, Storm would want to stay there forever, and that the day ahead of us was leading to perfection. I was wrong.

We walked along the path all the way down to the center of the park. We passed by beautifully colored birds who seemed to chirp love songs. The sun was shining and I knew with this weather the bright rays would hit the crystal, making it glow even stronger than usual. The sun was always shining on Storm, like it was a spotlight. It was as if someone was telling me that I should take note of this amazing person I have in front of me.

I knew that Storm and I were alike, and because I loved the crystal, I expected him to. Honestly, everyone loves it. People from other places always say they never see anything that glows. They call our island, "magical" but it's really quite normal to me. I think they just don't have crystals like ours, so they're not used to it.

But still, I wanted Storm to love it, because I did. I felt that it was one of my prized possessions, and I wanted to share it with him. After our kiss, all I could think about was making him happy. I had his smile on repeat in my brain, but I craved to see it in real life. I knew the crystal could bring it back.

When we arrived at the grand finale, what I saw horrified me. Earlier, as we walked towards it, I had noticed people looking frantic and concerned, but I didn't think much of it. Maybe it was because my head was in the clouds. A boy like Storm does that to you. When I got to the crystal, I understood. The iridescent crystal I'd loved was faded and gray. In all of my years living here, I have never, ever seen this happen. The only time I've even heard of it, was in the myth I'd mentioned before, about the man that couldn't dream. But that was always just a story, and I could have never imagined the only thing in my life that's ever been constant, to change. Storm looked confused too.

"Storm, we need to get back to my house. Something has gone terribly wrong."

"What's going on Jade?"

"It's the crystal. It's not supposed to be like this. It's supposed to be bright and glowing, it's supposed to show you the overall dream of the night, the mood of the town. It's supposed to be strong, it's supposed to draw you in. It's not supposed to be like this."

Storm looked deeply upset. I don't know why, it should have been me who was upset, not him. This crystal is everything to me and he doesn't even know what it is. But the look on his face was what I could've pictured his face to look like when his father died. I guess I was too shocked to ask. I couldn't help myself; my entire life had been flipped upside down. What was going on? As we rushed home I kept saying,

"It's not supposed to be like this. It's not supposed to be like this. It's not supposed to be like this."

Chapter 11

I knew this would happen. I knew I'd have to face this lilac envelope at some point or another, but I always thought I'd be doing it alone. I guess it makes sense to open it now, considering we're looking for my mom and this is pretty much the only clue we have, but I don't want to. And I most certainly didn't want Colby to find it. After I explained what the letter was, Colby was not happy.

"Really Lily? So, here I am, spending my time and energy trying to help YOU find YOUR mom, and you're keeping secrets from me. Weren't we just talking about how we were stumped, and we barely have any clues to find your mom. You just sat there, Lily. Did you not think you could trust me? I realize I didn't exactly prove I was trustworthy after the whole telling my dad about the journal and it getting out to the media because of that, but I thought we were past that."

"Colby, we are. We totally are. It's not trust that kept me from it. Honestly, I just didn't want to deal. Don't you think if it were easy I would've opened this envelope up the day I found it?"

"Lily, I get it, it's hard dealing with your mom. But I'm sick of all of this hesitation. You told me you were down to find her, and it seems like I'm the only one who's actually doing anything."

"Are you kidding me? Did you have an extremely uncomfortable talk with my dad about her?"

"No, but I forced you to. I get that you didn't want to think about your mom, so you didn't open the envelope before, but we're thinking about her now. You have to face this Lily, you have to just dive right in. You can't just stay at the surface and expect to find her. It's not going to be easy. But if you have information, like this, you can't be keeping it from me."

"Colby, why do you care so much? You need to stop telling me what to do and butt out. This is MY life. You clearly don't understand where I'm coming from, even though you seem to think you do. So, I slipped up, and forgot to tell you about the letter, but that does not give you the right to be telling me you're 'sick of the hesitation' I have. I really thought you were cooler than this Colby."

"And I really thought you wanted to find your mom."

"Get out of my house."

As he left I kept my head down so he wouldn't see the tears falling. I need to keep it together in front of him; it's so easy for him to rip me apart and he doesn't even see how vulnerable I am. At this point, I'm pretty sure this investigation is done. It's not like I ever wanted to do it anyway, and I'm sick of being pressured.

The way Colby blew up at me, it scared me. Why are both of the men in my life, and the closest people I have, questioning my ambitions and abilities to find my mom? Sure, I'm not exactly throwing myself into this head on, but it's not easy. I've tried to explain that to Colby, and I thought my dad would understand, which he pretty much has since our fight. I knew Colby was just too far away from my world to understand where I'm coming from.

But a mother is not a toy, she's not something I've simply lost and want to find. She's someone whose presence, and lack there of, have completely shaped who I am. I've thought about her ever since she's been gone, even when I don't realize it. This whole thing is going to end up changing MY life, not Colby's. It's just a game for him, an adventure, but it's my life he's playing with, and I'm not okay with being a puppet in his fun little attempt at detective.

The problem is, the letter's just sitting on my bed, and I'm pretty sure it's calling my name. Or, maybe it's calling "Ryan" but either way, the call is for me. I've thought about this letter a million times before, but I've never been this close to actually uncovering what's inside.

If I leave it alone, I'll never find her. Though I wasn't sure if this is what I wanted, I'm beginning to realize I really do want to see her, I just want to do it on my terms. If I open it though, I'll have to tell Colby. I'll have to call him, and apologize, and I'll feel stupid explaining to him that he's the reason why I opened it. But if I don't open it, I can go back to my life, and maybe I can open it later with Colby. He's always the strength of the team, and I'm not exactly sure I can do this by myself. But I have to; this is *my* mom. This is *my* life. If I want control of our search, I need to start being more independent.

Independence is so much easier said then done. As I hold the letter, I can't stop shaking. I feel every line on the outside of the envelope, brushing my finger along the curvy lines she once wrote. Ryan. Who is Ryan? Why did she leave me this? Did she know she wasn't coming back? Without even thinking, my finger slips under the seam of the seal. I'm careful to open it; I want to feel every part of the letter. I can't believe I'm pulling apart something my own mother once closed herself. It makes her feel real, and makes me feel closer to her.

She has beautiful handwriting. It's swirly and elegant; the handwriting of any teenage girl's dream. The one we use when we want to impress someone, even if it takes a lot longer to do. The one the popular girls have, and the girls like me envy. I don't know if I can read this.

What if it says something I don't want to hear? What if she's not who I want her to be? What if she just didn't really love my father and I? I look down at my trembling hands and see the ring my mother once wore. I don't know where she got it, and what it meant to her, but it gives me the ability to embrace another piece of her that I didn't have before. The stones on the ring are strong and stand bravely on my bony hands. She

wanted me to read this, and I'm old
enough now to do it.

To My Beautiful Daughter Ryan,
Wow! Daughter! I didn't think
I'd be saying that any time soon.
Trust me, if I knew, I would have
been more responsible about my
circumstances in America, and my
circumstances back home. But
don't take that the wrong way, you
are in NO means a regret of mine.
In fact, you're the most amazing
thing that has ever happened to me.
If you're reading this, that means
I'm not with you. I'm sorry I had to
leave Ryan, I would give anything
to stay here with you, but I can't.
And I wish I could've taken you and
your father with me, you two are the
reason I feel confident in my
knowledge of love and happiness in
this world. But for right now,
everything is too dangerous for you.
It's all very complicated, and
not exactly something I'm keen on
explaining over paper and pen. I
wish I could see you, and I could
hold you once again, so I could tell
you fully where I'm from and what
I'm doing home. Trust me, it's all in

good reason; I wouldn't leave you that easily.

I hope your father told you about me. I hope he still remembers me, and thinks about me, because I know I'll be thinking of him the entire time I'm gone. I hope you liked the journal. It's pretty cool isn't it, the world Storm and Jade lived in, and the things they got to see? And the love story too, it's quite moving. You're probably wondering why I gave it to you, and why I had it in the first place. I hope you've felt a connection to it, considering the words on those pages are running through your blood. I can't even explain to you how many times I've read it, how many times I've been amazed by what País de los Sueños used to be, and all of the beautiful sights it possessed. I hope some day it will be safe for you to come visit me there.

It's already hard writing this, and I haven't even left yet. I don't want you to think leaving is easy for me, or that I'll forget about you. Believe me when I say you are truly the light of my life, and the distance doesn't distract me from my

everlasting love for my daughter
Ryan. You'll always be on my mind,
and I hope you take me with you
wherever you go, in your heart at
least.

 Love forever and ever and ever
and ever,
  Ariella or Mom

My mom used to live in the Lost Land. Oh. My. God.

Chapter 12

Dear Revista,

Last night was awful. The worst part was the confusion I still have. When I rushed into my house my parents were first very concerned because they saw the look on my face. Then when I told them what had happened to the crystal, they looked at each other, then me, then Storm, and then told me I needed to go to my room.

I sat in my room freaking out; clearly whatever was happening was serious. I wanted my parents to assure me. I wanted my dad to laugh at me and my imagination, and pat me on the shoulder. I wanted my mom to put on her warm and welcoming smile and hug me. Even though I knew that I wasn't imagining this issue, I was hoping my parents would make me feel better about it. That whatever was happening, we would all stand together. Storm, too, since he's become a part of our family now, even though that's kind of weird, because he's also the object of my affection.

The weirdest part of my night though was that I was the only one that had to go to my room. Storm stayed in the kitchen with my parents. While I was exiled to face my fears on my own, Storm stayed up all night chatting with my mom and dad.

I'm done with all of these secrets. It's not hard to see that whatever is happening, Storm is either the cause of it, or he's knows why. He wouldn't just randomly show up in País de los Sueños and then this tragedy would magically happen. This is not a coincidence, and I'm getting to the bottom of it.

Storm made me feel like he had feelings for me, and I'm testing them today. Big surprise, my parents are busy. This time it's not with class, but they're meeting with the hadas about the crystal. They ordered me to take Storm on a hike in Mich Montañas, the mountain range here on País de los Sueños. I've never taken Storm here; I kind of disregard them. They're really far away from everything else on the island and I haven't been there in years.

When Storm finally came out of bed this morning he was groggy and quiet. I knew why, but. I just wanted to get today over with. I was getting answers, or there were going to be consequences. I'm not sure what they are, but I'm not dealing with the secrets anymore.

The whole walk to the mountains was quiet. Storm said he was tired, and just couldn't really deal. He didn't want to put any more stress on me than this catastrophe already had.

Luckily, I had the mountains to look at to ease my stress. I forgot how beautiful they were while I was drooling over the crystal in the park. I should've gone there more often, it would have been a great place to clear my mind. It's not like I'd have deep thoughts, it didn't really seem

*like a reflective kind of place, it'd
just distract me from my life.*

*The mountains were enormous, I
thought for sure the tips would reach
the sun. The landscape was
beautiful. The trees and flowers
danced on the earth like ballerinas
performing for the audience; us. But
even the views couldn't fully distract
me from Storm. We stopped at the
top of one of Mich's smaller
mountains and I had just about had
enough of our silent hike.*

*"Storm, we need to talk. I know you
know something about what's
happening to the crystals. You
probably know a lot of things,
considering you were able to spend
hours talking to my parents about it.
I'm sick of being left out of all of
these decisions. I was a part of this
family long before we even knew you
existed and I feel like I have the right
to be in on whatever is happening."*

*"You're absolutely right, Jade. I'm
sorry that I'm causing you stress, I
really am. If I knew I was going to
cause problems, I never would have*

come. I hate to see you upset, and it's time I give you an explanation to who I am, and what is happening. This has all gone too far."

"What's gone to far?"

"I told you my father died, and that he wasn't welcome here. You said that was crazy, that everyone is welcome here, but Jade, you and I both know there was one man that was not."

"You're not telling me…"

"Yes, I am. The myth, the nightmare, he is, or was my father. You know he couldn't dream, and the hadas didn't like him. He was a distraction for them. They had conferences on what to do with him and at the final one, instead of asking him to leave, they kidnapped him. My father was strong willed like I told you, though he didn't believe in himself fully, he had bravery running through his veins. He didn't want to leave his new home, he saw the beauty here that I have been lucky enough to see, and he wanted to stay. The hadas didn't

like his refusal, and they imprisoned him, leaving him to die."

"The hadas wouldn't do that Storm. They're great fairies. They've done nothing but made País de los Sueños a paradise for my family, and for everyone we know. Why did you say he was a distraction for them? I know he couldn't dream, but so what?"

"That's the thing. This is why I didn't want to tell you. I know you love it here Jade, and I wouldn't want to give you a bad impression on everything here, but there are things you need to know. The hadas are planning something awful, and I'm afraid I'm already too late. The crystal is not just a portrayal of the dreams of the night, but the brightness and purity of it gives the hadas power. They feed off of the strength of the dreams, and store their power inside of the crystal. Jade, they're planning to take over other nations and countries once they get enough power here, and create more crystals, and towns surrounding it, like this one."

"You make them seem like villains, Storm. País de los Sueños is great, what would be the big deal if more places were modeled after it?"

"If the hadas can turn the world into one that is surrounded by a crystal, and supported by them, they ultimately have all of the power. Power is never a good thing, Jade. Everyone will become dependent on them, and what they provide, and soon enough they'll be able to control and manipulate others into what they want. The hadas are leading us to world destruction, and they must be stopped."

"Storm, you can't just come in here, and tell me that my beautiful home is actually the brains to a plan to take over the world. How dare you rip apart everything I know and love?"

"Jade, I'm sorry it has to be like this. Initially, I thought I could come here, and stop them myself. I thought I wouldn't have to tell you, or any of your people about their evil ways. You'd never have to lose the hope

you've surrounded your life with. But the hadas are already very powerful, Jade. I couldn't do it alone, and it's gotten to a point where they've noticed my presence."

"So, you're the reason why the crystal is dull?"

"Sadly, yes. I didn't know it would be like this. Your parents told me there was a good chance I wouldn't be able to dream either, but I've been spending a lot of time in classes, trying to learn. Your parents are great teachers, Jade, but I'm a special case."

"You mean, my parents knew about you? They knew who you were? And what you were here for? They knew who the hadas were, and what they were doing?"

"They were helping me Jade. They were helping you too."

"This all makes so much sense. How could you all go behind my back like this? Storm, this is my family, my home, and you've completely turned

it upside down. Everything I've ever known, the two people I trust the most, everything is a lie. I want you to go home. I need to go home."

"I can't go back. I need to hide from the hadas. They're dangerous, and I can only help if I'm not under their control."

"Well, you can hide alone, Storm. I don't know who to trust, or where to go, but it's not going to be here with you."

"Jade, please, don't leave me here. I'll be able to go back in a few hours, when your parents are done with the hadas, but for now I need to be here, and I'd really like it if you were too. I understand you're mad, you have every right to be, but don't leave me Jade. Please."

How could I resist Storm? His hazel eyes were glistening with tears that began to roll down his sun kissed cheeks. I wanted to kiss them away, make him feel better, but I also wanted him to cry. I wanted him to feel some of the emotions I was experiencing.

"Fine, but I'm not talking to you. I need time to think."

"Jade, you're truly amazing."

So in summary, Storm is the son of the man who couldn't dream. And guess what? Storm can't dream either. And the whole reason he is here is because the hadas, the creatures I've always looked up to and admired, are actually evil and planning to take over the world. In fact, that's going to happen pretty soon. And my parents, who are also my best friends, (I realize that sounds lame), have known about Storm and the hadas the entire time, but just didn't tell me. Now, more then ever, I just want to get away from País de los Sueños. This time, I never want to come back.

Chapter 13

I cannot wrap my head around this. My mom, Ariella Dorlin, lived in País de los Sueños, or as the rest of the world knows it, The Lost Land. All of these years I'd pictured her doing different things in different places, but not once did I imagine her there. Colby was right: I am connected to the book. I wonder how my mom got it; who is Jade? I wonder if she knew Jade.

Colby would freak out if I told him. I'm freaking out too. But I'm not telling him yet. I'm not so comfortable with the way he handled this search for my mom before, and it seems like the more he finds out the more prodding he does. After thinking over our fight, I do understand where he's coming from. I don't agree with his ignorance towards my feelings, but I should have told him about the letter. I never really thought about it connecting to me finding my mom. I only ever think about it when I'm reading the book and I see the corner peeking out from the ends of the journal. I never realized it would reveal this much about my mother.

Even with her location, I still have so many questions for her. She never talked about the danger she had to return to, and it's not like the journal ever really finished the story. She also never talked about who Storm and Jade were. What if Jade is a code name and Ariella is really Jade? What if there was no danger, what if she was going back to be with Storm, her one true love? I guess I can't think that way. I felt the sincerity in her voice when she talked about how much she cared about me, which she did a lot, and I'm going to stand by it. I have more confidence in the love my mother once had for me, and potentially still does. That doesn't mean I'm satisfied with her just yet. I need to know more.

Sadly, the only way I see myself opening up doors is by going back to my dad. I feel like it's going to cause problems because we just got over the first extravaganza, and he told me he wasn't emotionally ready to deal with the subject of my mother. Every time we talk about her, it never exactly ends well, but if it means finding her, I'm willing to fight. Take that Colby, your girl's being independent without any guidance from you!

The problem with talking to my dad is that he doesn't know about the book. When the media frenzy happened he was away on a business trip, and by the time he came back the calls had started to thin out until I stopped getting them. I'm nervous he's going to get mad that I kept this from him. I know he misses my mom just as much, if not more than I do, and he probably would have loved to have this piece of her with him, even if I'm not sure if it's really a piece of her. Maybe I am selfish. He lost his one true love and I've been harboring this journal from him and the world. I wonder if he reads it, will he know some of the things they're saying? Will he be able to tell me how Ariella connects?

I have to tell him. I wish I had the confidence Colby has. I don't know if I can do this. But if I don't, I'll be back to square one trying to find my mom. And I know if I tell Colby about the letter, the next step will be to talk to my dad. I have to do this. It's like ripping off a band-aid. I can't sit here and wait, my mom's not coming to find me. It's now or never.

"Hey Dad, could you come in here?"

"Yeah, one second Lil."

Shoot, maybe I shouldn't tell him. What is he going to say? What if he knows about the book?

"What's up?"

"I know you told me you didn't really want to be involved in the whole "Search for Mom" project, but I need to ask you something. Well, I guess I need to tell you something."

"Okay, what is it?"

"Well, mom left me a book, and a letter. I never opened the letter before, until today, but I thought you might like to see it, and maybe if you read it you'll be able to tell me more about her."

I handed him the letter with shaking hands. He was frowning at first, but as he started to read, teardrops fell. He sat down next to me with watery eyes.

"Oh, Ariella. I miss her every day, Lily. Maybe I should start calling you Ryan, I think she'd want that."

"Dad, I'm pretty sure if you call me Lily, she's not going to know. I think she'd be happy with me finding my independence and being my own person."

"Lily, this letter is beautiful. Thank you for sharing it with me. But I'm confused, what is the journal she's talking about? What's her 'land?'"

"Well, Dad, that's the other part. I've been keeping something kind of important from you, and from everyone I guess. Unfortunately, everyone now knows about it, and that's pretty much what kick started my search for Mom. It's a journal of a girl who used to live in the Lost Land. It was actually called País de los Sueños. It's the story of what happened to it, and Mom left it for me when she went back to her home. I never really thought it was that big a deal, but when you were away, news channels and writers were practically beating down the door to get a look at the book."

"Alright, first of all Lily, why didn't you call me? If people were bothering you while I was gone I would have rushed home to be with you, even if I didn't know why. You know that. Second of all, well I don't really know what to say. Your mother lived there, in the Lost Land? And I can't believe you had the key to it and you've never said anything."

"Dad, how was I supposed to know it was real? Maybe I shouldn't have told you—"

"No, Lily I'm really happy you told me. If it's all right with you, I'd like to read the journal. I mean, I know you want me to help, but I know nothing about it."

"Well, sure. But I'd like to talk about it when you're done."

"Does Colby know about this?"

"Not about the letter, necessarily."

He took the book and went to his room. I hope somehow this helps me find my mom, because it's beginning to seem like my dad is losing faith in me. Just as I was ready to call Colby, my dad called from his room,

"Lily! I need you in here."

I ran in and his eyes were huge.

"Lily, Ariella's mom was named Jade."

Chapter 14

Dear Revista,

I honestly don't know how I feel. Yesterday, my whole life was flipped upside down and I've never felt more betrayed. I've never felt so alone. I realize that Storm needs me to be there for him, and my parents need to support him too, but I've also always had trust in the hadas, and now my closest relatives and friends are telling me to go against them.

When Storm and I finally got back home last night, which was way after the sun went down, the creases that surrounded my mothers mouth moved to burden her forehead. My father also looked concerned, but Storm was the worst. I didn't really understand why, I mean sure País de los Sueños and its' safety was the dying wish of his father, but it's been my family's home since before we can trace. It's all we know, and we're going against it. My mom and dad saw my confusion and then explained to me that Storm's life was in grave danger. He is not only ruining the aura of the crystal, but he's turning people against the hadas. Since we've already been turned, our lives are in danger too. Great, this just gets better and better.

"Mom, how do they know we're on Storm's side? And how do they know we even know him?"

"Well, they don't know for sure, but they know we've been demanding more food lately, and they know that Storm has to be somewhere on the island."

"But so? He could be anywhere, and maybe I'm gaining weight, or you're pregnant. Did you tell them that?"

"Well, Sweetie, there is a slight problem."

I just couldn't wait to hear how this whole thing got worse. But it was my dad who looked up with saddened, gray eyes, and said,

"Yesterday as the hadas were leaving, one of them noticed a

teenage boy's pair of pants in the laundry basket. They freaked out and asked whose they were. I tried to say they were mine, but they didn't believe me, so we said you had a boyfriend and he left them here. They said they believed it, but they still took the pants with them for 'investigation purposes.' They can't prove our involvement, but they want Storm gone."

For the second time in two days Storm started crying. His father thought he was strong and courageous, and I did too, but his wall had fallen. Storm was scared, and I don't blame him. I'm scared too, and it's worse for him. My parents had to leave to teach a class, since it would be suspicious if they stopped their lives because of this problem, and now more then ever País de los Sueños needed strong dreams.

"Jade, I want you to know that whatever happens, I'm terribly sorry for my disruption. And I want you to know how I feel. I think you're so lovely. Do you know that? You're

*just like one of Casara's flowers.
Your beauty is delicate but you're so
strong. You may not think you are,
but you are. At first, flowers are
closed. If you leave them alone, they
stay closed and eventually wither
away. But if you take the time to care
for flowers, they blossom and give
you much more than you could ever
ask for. I've watched you blossom
before me and I can't thank you
enough. Please know if I don't make
it out, you deserve the best."*

*"Storm, it's going to be okay.
Seriously, my parents are basically
royalty on this island, they'll be able
to settle this; they always do."*

*"Jade, I don't think you understand
the intensity of the situation. The
hadas have had this plan for many
years, which means they've had
many years to build up their power."*

*"I don't think you understand,
actually. Though I didn't know the
evil that the hadas possessed, I have
known them my entire life. And I've
known this island my entire life. My
parents have never failed to be my*

heroes, even now, and if I'm confident not to question their abilities, you should be too."

"But Jade, your parents have never actually had to face this problem head on. Soon, something is going to come of my presence on the island, and most likely it will be my death. I just want you to know that no matter what happens to me, I can't explain how much I appreciate what your family has done. Your parents are brave, and so are you. But you're more then brave Jade; you're beautiful, smart, caring, and you're the first girl I've ever fallen this hard for—"

Then he started crying and excused himself to go to his room. I just don't know what to say, Revista. I've fallen for him too, and it sickens me to hear him talk about dying, or something bad happening. Life on the island has always been simple and sweet, and I wish it could stay that way. I'm not sure how to deal with a problem like this.

Maybe this is why I need to travel more. So I can see the problems the world faces, and understand how others react. Maybe, I'll even be able to help them. I mean, I'm helping Storm, and my parents have helped so many people all their lives. Maybe helping others is in my blood, but I'll never know unless I see what is out there for me.

But how could I be thinking about my future right now when Storm is predicting that he won't have one? I can't believe I'm being so selfish. I should go find him, and tell him I feel the same, and that I'm in this fight side by side with him.

My dad just called my name and asked if Storm was in here with me. Why would he be in my room alone with me? Hold on.

Revista, I'm not sure if I should freak out, but my parents can't find Storm. They hadn't seen him for a while, and assumed we were hanging out so they didn't say anything. But I haven't seen him for a while either. He could be blowing off some steam, trying to get his mind away from his troubles. But who am I kidding? Storm just lectured me in the mountains about how he couldn't be alone. This is bad, this is very, very bad. I think I know where Storm is, but it's not going to be easy getting him back. Everyone was right all along, this battle is too big for me.

Chapter 15

Jade is my grandmother. I don't think I'd believe it even if Jade came back to life and told me herself. The whole time I've been reading this journal, this journal of a mysterious and amazingly adventurous girl, I've been reading about my grandmother. Jade, the girl who grew up on País de los Sueños, who stared into the flowing water of Charriet's Fountain, who played on the beaches of La Playa de Greel, who felt the delicate flower petals from Casara's on her fingertips, who went to the park and the mountains, and who kissed Storm in the water at Estrella's.

And Storm! Is Storm my grandfather? I really hope he is. But Jade and Storm were just teenagers when they met, and Storm was such a hassle for Jade with all of the trouble he caused. My dad doesn't know what Ariella's dad's name was, he only knew Jade. I wonder if I could be the grandchild of Storm and Jade. That would be magical. To know my grandparents lived the lives they did, and to know their love story like the back of my hand, well that would just be a dream.

Dad can't get to sleep and neither can I. He's freaking out about the book in general. I'm freaking out about Jade. Dad isn't even really commenting on the fact that now I know who my grandmother is, because he's too busy with the whole story of the book. I never really remember that the book uncovers the secret behind the lost land and what happened to it because it's always just been a story. Just a story, now a part of my history.

I wish my dad would stop studying the pages and listen to me because I want to talk about my grandmother. I want to describe her with all of her beauty and be able to say, "That's my grandma." He doesn't even really care that much because he doesn't know Jade that well. I can see how this whole thing can be a little overwhelming for him, but I'm pretty overwhelmed myself.

This means that I'm a descendant from the Lost Land! My grandmother was a brave and beautiful woman with a courageous soul and she lived in País de los Sueños. I want to go there, to see where she was from, and walk the land she walked on.

I should tell Colby. He would listen. He would be so excited, too. He'd probably think I was really cool. Yes, I should definitely tell Colby. But maybe not today. My dad is completely flabbergasted with what he read that he continues to reread the entire thing again and again and I have a feeling I'm going to be spending some time explaining to him the story behind the book and how I got it, again.

No longer can I contain my anger towards Colby and his ignorance. We all have flaws; I'm not perfect either, and I think it's time for Colby to be clued in. He doesn't even know that Ariella lived in the Lost Land. I'm excited and nervous to see his reaction. He's really determined and I know with all of this new information he'll figure some more stuff out. And when my dad gets over his hump of astonishment, he can help me too.

This is all coming together. For the first time in my life I actually feel like I'll be able to find my mom.

Chapter 16

Dear Revista,

When I told my parents that Storm had been kidnapped by the hadas I was almost surprised at how easily they believed me. Though I had thought it, and said it out loud, I didn't want to believe it. I've always seen my parents in a positive light and know I have to accept them for who they really are but it's so hard to just turn around and do that. That's like if someone said, "Your mom actually hates you and is planning to give you up for adoption." That would be way to hard to believe and take some serious convincing.

My parents said the only way of saving our land and our new friend Storm would be to get him back.

"Get him back? What do you mean?"

"We mean we need to kidnap him back, Jade. Your mother and I have

a good feeling about where they're keeping him because we know their lair like the back of our hands. You know the cave that's near the crystal in the park? The one that the hadas always fly in and out of?"

"Storm is in the park?"

"Well, that's what we were thinking. Your father brought up a good point, that the hadas would want to keep Storm close to the crystal to be a reminder about what he is doing and to prove that he's the one doing it, before they take any serious action. But we don't have much time, we need to get him back."

"But mom, what happens if we do? They're just going to come looking for him again."

"Sweetie, once we get Storm back, you need to prepare to fight."

"Fight the hadas? No! I'm sorry but this has all gone too far. Why can't we just leave, go to the America, or Australia, or Africa; anywhere! We can't fight the hadas."

"What we can't do is leave our home behind to be destroyed by the hadas. Jade, they're getting more and more powerful as days go on and if we leave, we'll leave our country in jeopardy. Soon enough the hadas will take over and start coming for other parts of the world. This is inevitable; it's time to face them."

"But Dad—"

I just started crying. Crying because I was sad, that the hadas I once looked up to were terribly evil creatures who wanted to destroy me. Crying because the boy I think I love is in grave danger of being killed, and I'm going to have to kidnap him back which puts me in danger. Crying because either way the life I knew and loved was changing. And crying because I knew my parents were right. We couldn't leave behind this problem, it was our role to step up and face this head on.

"I'm just scared."

"Sweetie, it's okay. You're strong and smart and we won't be fighting alone."

"We won't?"

"Of course not! Your mother and I have been rounding up as many people who will believe us, and we are preparing them for war. We could never do this alone, but luckily we don't have to."

"Wow, other people want to fight too?"

"Not necessarily want, but they see the dire need. But enough about that, we need to focus on getting Storm back."

"What do you plan on doing?"

"Well, we were thinking your mother could just take you to the park with her to look at the crystal, like the many times before. This time, you start screaming in terror about the color or lack of it, and gathering people to ask about what is happening to the island. By causing

a scene, you'll distract the hadas, and your mom will sneak in and find him."

"Mom, that's so dangerous. What if you get hurt? What if they kill you too?"

"Don't think that way Jade. It will all run smoothly. The hadas don't expect us to be fighting against them; we do business with them. This plan is fool proof."

Except the plan is not fool proof. My parents may think I have the wildest imagination on the island, but I could not say the same for them. If the hadas were as powerful as everyone keeps telling me, there's going to be a catch. It can't be that easy.

As I write this, I realize I'm going to need to go and get him myself. It's the only way. I would rather put myself in danger than my mother and I know somehow I can do this, I feel it in my bones. I have motive to get Storm back. This is just a fight for País de los Sueños to my

*parents, but this is a fight for a home
and my love. I don't know how, but I
know tonight when my parents go to
sleep, I'll go. It has to be me.*

Chapter 17

Colby just rang the doorbell. I think he thinks I'm still mad at him, and that I'm having him come over to apologize, but that is seriously not the case. I can't wait to see what he has to say about all of this new information. I can't wait to see his bright blue eyes light up with excitement.

"Hey."

He said, in a solemn voice. His eyes were not bright, they were dull. This is so unlike him.

"What's up Colbs? You seem like something is wrong."

"Something is wrong Lily. I can't deal with you being mad at me. I've literally been sitting in my house like a couch potato just staring at the wall. My mom couldn't even get me to watch American Idol, and you know that show is my secret weakness. I wanted to come over, but I didn't know how to apologize. I want to make sure that what I say is perfect, and that I never mess up again. This search for your mom has been the most exciting thing in my entire life; I don't think you realize that. Spending all of this time with you has been amazing and adventurous and I really don't want it to end. I'm sorry I can't think of anything to say but I hope you hear the sincerity in my voice and find it in your heart to forgive me."

I started laughing and Colby went from sad puppy dog to really confused.

"Colby, you were wrong. Very wrong. But so was I. I'm not harboring any anger over what happened between us because I don't have time. And because I missed you. I have so much to tell you. You're going to freak out!"

Just like that he was back to the old Colby I knew and loved. His eyes lit up and his smile brightened my entire house. I could just melt in his smile; his perfect white teeth and the dimples that become visible when he's really happy. This kid has such a grasp on me. I should be more mad than I am, but after Colby looked so sad about not being around me, my knees weakened and all was forgiven. I know he'll never use his good looks as a power over me though, at least not that much.

"So, what did you want to tell me? I can't wait to hear it!"

"Okay, my mom, she used to live in the Lost Land."

The color from his face drained with excitement. He looked shocked, and surprised, and happy. I decided instead of just explaining everything to him, I'd let him read the letter. This time I wasn't handing it over with shaky hands, but with proud ones. As I read the letter more and more I realized my mother loves me so much, and I'm going to find her soon and prove that to anyone who questions it.

"Oh. My. God."

Colby's freaking out, just like I knew he would.

"She said 'my land.' Lily, you are basically from País de los Sueños. I can't believe this. She keeps saying you're connected to the book. I knew it! I told you!"

"Well, that's the other thing. After reading that, I knew I had to talk to my dad. And be proud, because I actually did, by myself, no coaching from you. After explanations and introductions to the book and letter from my mom, I finally got my dad settled and ready to read it. When he opened up the first page and noticed it was signed, 'Jade,' he informed me that my grandmothers name was Jade. Colby, Jade is my grandmother."

Once again I've never seen the boy this pale. His skin is always caramel colored with a fresh tint. I couldn't tell you how, we're surrounded by tall skyscrapers here in New York that tend to shade any sun coming our way, but Colby has a way to make anything and everything work out for him.

"Oh my God, Lily. Wait, if Jade is your grandma, is Storm your grandpa?"

"I don't know! I don't really know anything. But from my mom's letter, I know that when she left us she went back to País de los Sueños. I think she may still be there."

"Then we have to go, Lily! Let's leave now! You have the map, we can do it!"

"Well, I want to, but I have to talk to my dad."

Why did I say I want to? I had never even thought about actually going to País de los Sueños. It's probably hard to find considering nobody ever has before, and I'm almost positive my dad is not going to let me go. But I want to, if it means finding my mom, I really want to.

"Dad, can you come in here?"

"Yeah, what's up?"

He says as he pokes his head through the door.

"Oh, hey Colby."

"Hey Mr. D"

"Dad, you know how I showed you the letter mom wrote me. Well it seemed like when she left she went back to País de los Sueños, and I think she still may be there. Colby and I were thinking we should go. It's summer, so we don't have school or anything, and if it means finding Mom I want to go."

"You must be joking. You and Colby, going to the Lost Land, where no one has ever been, alone? Not going to happen."

What was up with his harsh tones? Why did he have to shoot me down so quickly?

"Well, you could come too! Then you'd be able to see her. And it's not like no one's ever gone Dad, obviously Mom has been. You said you'd support me but it really doesn't feel like that."

"Honey, I'll support you in searching for her, but I'm not letting you take off to a foreign and mysterious island with your friend to find your mother when we really have no idea where she is. You have to understand how irrational you're being."

"Can you stop attacking me? That's all you ever do, Dad. You just tear me apart. I have hopes of finding her and I finally know where she is and you're keeping me away. I know you said you didn't want to be a part of this, but you are so get over it. This is my mother, and she may not mean anything to you but she sure as hell means something to me."

Colby shifted uncomfortably. I turned the ruby ring around my finger over and over again, focusing on the rhythmic movement.

"Don't you dare tell me your mother didn't mean anything to me. You don't know anything about us."

He stormed out of the room and that was it. I wish that my dad and I could have normal conversations, but that just wasn't going to happen I guess.

"Colby, we're going to the Lost Land. No objections. I don't care what he said, if he doesn't want me to go, then he doesn't have to know. Go home and get ready, I'll meet you tonight at 10 outside of my apartment."

Colby smiled like he was really proud of me. Maybe his adventurous spirit is rubbing off on me, or maybe I really want to see my mom. Either way, once I step off of this cliff and head towards my mom, I know all hell will break loose.

Chapter 18

Dear Revista,

Last night when I heard both of my parent's soft lull of sleep coming from their rooms, I left my house. It was the most terrifying thing in the world to me. My parents told me we wouldn't be fighting alone but in a way, I was.

Though the crystal was black the iridescent glow still illuminated the park lightly along with the stars. I crept quietly past the place that had once been nothing but peace to me, and found the cave my parents had been talking about. Sure enough, the hadas were inside, I saw the glow from their bodies shining out of the entrance. I waited until it got later and later and the lighting from their bodies started to fade as they got farther away from the entrance of the cave. I could tell from how bright the light was, that there was only one remaining in the front of the cave, and if I was quiet enough, I could go unseen.

I snuck right up close to it and realized that the final glow I had been seeing had not been a hada, but the glow from the bars holding Storm. His cage was cursed. By what, I didn't know.

"Storm, it's me. How are you? Are you hurt? What did they put on your cage?"

"Jade, get out of here before they see you! This is far too dangerous for you. You can't be here I won't let you go down with me."

"Storm, please, I'm your last chance. You know I'm not going away. Just answer my questions."

I pleaded quietly with him and the silence in the air was louder then I'd ever heard before. Finally, he said,

"I'm not hurt but I feel weak. The cage is locked with the curse of my bad dreams. It's slowly pulling out all of the forms of dreams I've ever had. It's powered by dreams, like

everything else in this island, Jade. I have no idea how it unlocks, but I don't have much time. I'm getting weaker as it's getting stronger."

"Don't worry, I'll figure it out Storm. I'm a soñador, remember? My imagination runs miles."

Finally, my imagination would go to something of good use. I started circling the cage, looking for a door or a lock or something. There was nothing in sight. I could not imagine how they got him in, and how they planned on getting him out, if they even did. I could just picture Storm waiting in there for days as he was slowly weakened to the point where he couldn't stand, see, or talk. I wouldn't let that happen.

"Storm, I don't understand, how did they get you in here?"

"I don't know, they knocked me out and when I woke up I was here. Jade, please, go home. There's no way out. Dreams are always too powerful of a resource here."

"Wait! That's it! They locked you in with the curse of your bad dreams. They get their power from their dreams Storm. Maybe I have power from my dreams. What if I can unlock, or at least weaken the hold on your cage, with my dreams?"

"That's ridiculous Jade. You need to be home, not sleeping around this cave waiting for your dreams to unlock me while I sit here and witness a hada come and tear you apart."

"Storm, I can do this. I believe I can do it. I've been learning how to dream strongly my entire life. If anyone can dream to unlock you, it's me. Whether you like it or not, I'm here to stay, until your ready to leave. I need to find somewhere dark to sleep so I can do this without being seen."

"Jade, I don't doubt you dream with great strength, but I'm not letting you do this. I can't be the reason why something bad happens, and I won't be able to sit here and see it. Can you imagine how terrible it

would be to see the love of your life being hurt by something and you couldn't do anything about it?"

He said I was the love of his life.

"Yes, I can imagine it, because it's happening to me right now! Either help me find a dark place, or leave me to find one myself and possibly risk being found."

"Fine. The far corner away from the cage is the darkest because it's the farthest away from the illumination. I'm going to scream if any of them come in, and if you hear that, run. Don't look back, just get out of here alive and find your parents."

"Storm please don't say that. It'll be fine, this will be quick."

And with that I went to sleep. I remember the dream I had so vividly, it was as if it was real life, because it pretty much was. In my dreams I recalled my first kiss with Storm in the water: perfection. Then when we sat in the mountains together and I was mad at everyone but the feeling

*that overcame me was this horrible
fear that I'd lose him. Then when he
was saying goodbye, and that he
didn't want to cause me any
problems. After that, my imagination
started to work. I dreamt of Storm
and I getting out of the cave and
back to my parents. The hadas were
so stunned by his escape that they
froze where they were and we didn't
have to worry about fighting them
anymore because they weren't a
threat. My parents took over the
crystal instead of the hadas, and all
was well. Storm and I were able to
be happy together with no worries in
the world. Everything was—*

"AHHHHHH"

*I woke up to Storm screaming. I
quietly gasped in fear as my eyes
opened and I saw the hadas float
around his cage. It had worked! My
dreams had weakened the curse on
the bars, but the hadas noticed, and
were not happy. I knew that Storm
told me to run if I heard him, but I
couldn't leave him behind. My
dreams were working, I couldn't
stop. The hadas were still confused*

*but I knew that they'd go get a
bigger army before they actually did
anything about the cage. I floated
back to sleep and continued to dream
of Storm, his eyes, his hair, his body
at Estrella's in the water, the way he
cared about me.*

*Suddenly, something grabbed
me and woke me up. I was almost too
afraid to open my eyes but I heard,*

*"Jade, it worked. We need to get out
of here now."*

*Sure enough, Storm was holding
me in his arms, trying to drag me out
of the cave. I was so shocked that my
dreams worked, and that he had
woken me up, not the hadas, I wasn't
exactly quick on my feet. We sprinted
toward the entrance but I could
already feel the presence of a hada
behind us. The hada's glow flashed
with anger and illuminated the entire
cave, making both Storm and I
extremely visible. We ran, and ran,
and ran back to my house as the
hada got the rest of its army ready to
find us.*

As we arrived breathlessly into my house and woke my parents I realized, this was it, this was war.

Chapter 19

When I saw Colby's red jeep wrangler parked next to my building I almost screamed with excitement. I needed to get out of my house. My life was just one move after another, but always empty. It was time I filled the missing pieces. I left my dad a note saying that Colby and I were leaving and that when I find mom I'd come back for him. I'm mad at him but I'm also extremely scared to actually find her, especially without him by my side, and I don't want him to be worried about me on top of it. He's not going to be happy but I'm sure he'll forget about it when I walk through the door with Ariella.

"Get in Lily! It's now or never!"

I hopped up into the car and shivered with nerves. He drove off quickly because he knew I'd have second thoughts, but with Colby, it's hard to have second thoughts. He's just so sure about everything, and as he smiled at me I realized he could convince me to do anything, which was probably not a good thing.

But in some ways it was. I would never have searched for my mom without him, and I would definitely not be on my way to País de los Sueños without him. Speaking of which,

"So, Mr. Genius, how do you expect we get to País de los Sueños when it's in Mexico and we're in New York?"

Colby smiled and pointed to the back seat. I looked behind me and shrieked with fear as I saw a boy sitting there, also smiling. He wasn't exactly a boy, he was about 20, and extremely handsome. He had mocha colored hair and the same deep sea blue eyes that Colby did. Oh, this was Doug.

"Hi Doug, nice to meet you."

"How'd you know it was me? Colby, she's a keeper."

"Well, I've heard so much about you, and you guys could be twins so that's also a give away."

"Doug's here to take us to where he does his school work. He's going to help us study the map and figure out where exactly we need to go in order to get there."

"Lily, I think this whole thing is really cool. Maybe I could even make a copy of the map for my studies! Talk about an A+ when I walk into class with that thing!"

"No way are you making a copy, bro! This thing was clearly kept a secret for a reason. If they wanted people to go to País de los Sueños they would have welcomed others in. Who knows what happened to all of those who went looking for it but didn't return?"

The car got quiet. We never really discussed the dangers of finding País de los Sueños. There were countless reporters and historians who tried to find it, and never came back. What if that happened to Colby and I? I started turning the ring on my finger nervously. Doug decided to break the silence,

"What's País de los Sueños?"

"The Lost Land, Dude. Sorry Lil, I didn't exactly fill him in on all of the details."

We arrived at the classroom and it was really dark. Doug said he had a key and could get us in. His school was built right by the Long Island Sound and Colby was mesmerized by the reflection of the sunset on the water. Colby was a surfer at heart and used to go down to Florida every summer to stay with his grandma. He'd surf all day then come home and they'd have dinner together. She died last December and this was the first summer he didn't go. I can tell it's killing him being back by the water. I wish there was something I could do for him, but I can't bring back the dead.

All I can do is be here if he wants to talk about it, but he never does. He'll talk about anything but his grandma. It's okay though, I know the feeling of wanting to avoid that conversation with my mom. He'll talk when the time is right.

"Isn't it amazing? The marine bio departments take these boats out every day and collect stuff to look at. My classroom overlooks the water, so we see them all of the time. I think it'd be pretty cool to do that."

"They go out on these boats? These things are huge! They're like bigger than any of Dad's friends' boats."

"Yeah, it's crazy right? Some really rich guy's son went here and did the program and wasn't happy with it. He said they didn't have enough technology to please him, so the dad bought both of these boats with the latest and greatest technology, along with a new lab for them."

"Wow, sounds like some spoiled kid."

Colby sounded far away. I wondered if it was just the memories of his grandmother or it was something else. Either way, I could feel the moment becoming awkward.

"So, Doug, did you want to see my map or something?"

"Hell yeah! Let's go inside!"

We walked in but Colby lingered by the water. I can never tell what he's thinking but I didn't feel like it was the right time to ask. Doug was getting really excited as I handed him the map. He thought it was the coolest thing in the world and took forever to actually remember that he was trying to help us figure out how to get there.

Finally we figured out a plan. Doug told us we could fly down to Mexico and take a boat to the island. The island is right by Yucatan, which is somewhat close to the US, and taking a boat would be easy. He said at some point we're going to need to figure out some of the stuff on our own though, because it wouldn't be as easy as just taking a

boat down by Yucatan. If it were,
people would have already done it.

That makes me nervous. Why
has no one been there before? It's
not that far away from us. I'm just
hoping that if I show them the book
or prove to them that I belong there,
I'll be allowed on the island. If we
can even find it.

"Bro, do you have money for a plane
or something? I have a few bucks but
nothing to get you to Mexico. I mean
you guys could drive but it'd be a
pretty long—"

"I got it, don't worry."

Once again, Colby had a distant
look in his eye. I didn't know what
he was talking about but I hoped he
really did have it under control
because I didn't think to bring a lot
of money. I only have a small brown
satchel with the journal, the map, and
a few dollars, nothing special.

"Thanks, Doug, for showing us how
to do it! I promise when we get back
we'll show you the map again and

maybe let you copy it. Come on, Lily, let's go."

He grabbed my hand and quickly led me outside as we heard, "Uh, Bye! Nice meeting you!" faintly being called. Once again I was electrified by Colby's touch, for a moment it felt like he was whisking me away on a romantic vacation or something.

That moment was almost coming true when instead of leading me back to his car he started walking me toward the water. He said he wanted to show me something and sparks of excitement shocked my body. Was he going to talk about his grandmother and open up? Was he going to kiss me by the water? Was he going to show me pretty shells that reminded him of me?

No, he wasn't going to do any of that. We walked out on the dock quickly, and I heard the water sloshing under my feet. Colby told me he wanted to show me something really cool on one of the boats, something that could help us find

Yucatan quickly after we got to Mexico. He even lifted me up over the edge so I wouldn't get wet or anything when I was getting on. Then he hopped on. Doug came running out screaming,

"Dude, don't go on those things! They're like really expensive and I'm not even allowed on them!"

But it was too late. Colby had snagged keys for the boat while Doug and I were heading inside to look at the map and he started revving up the engine.

"Dude, what are you doing? Get off! I'm serious—"

But the sound of Doug's voice was muffled by the engine and the water as Colby quickly turned the boat around and motored down the sound. Fortunately, my voice could be heard.

"Colby, are you serious? You can't do this! This is stealing! This is crazy! We need to go back! We can find another way! We don't even have to go if you don't want! But we can't do this—"

I just kept screaming, trying desperately to get him to stop, but once we were clear of the land and all you could see was the water around us, he sat back on the captain's seat and started whooping.

"Colby, this is not funny!"

"Don't you feel alive Lily? I feel like I can do anything! We're on our way to get your mom! You shouldn't have any worries!"

"No worries? What about the fact that you just stole a boat? Or that you don't know how to drive a boat? Or that we don't know where we're going?"

"We can give the boat back after we're done, I'm not going to destroy it! My grandma taught me how to drive a boat when I was five years old. País de los Sueños is in your blood, but the ocean is in mine. It'll be fine Lily. Doug said this thing has the best technology. I'm sure it could practically steer itself to Yucatan. We have a map, we have technology, we have it all."

"What happens if we can't find it? What happens if we die on this boat? Then who's going to return it, Colby?"

His smile faded and he came over to where I was sitting. He hugged me and rubbed my back, saying,

"Lily, we're not going to die, we're going to find your mother. I won't rest until we find her. You deserve this."

And then he kissed me. Maybe because he thought we were going to die, and he didn't want to feel alone. Or maybe because he really liked me. But he kissed me. He kissed me! Oh my god! This is what I had wanted from day one with him, and it finally came true! Why can't I be more excited about it?

"Colby, you need to be paying attention to where we're going."

He looked at me with
uncertainty. I know he wanted me to
say something, anything, but I
couldn't. I was happy, I definitely
was, but I was scared. We'd stolen a
boat and our lives were in extreme
danger. I hope he understood that.
He went back to the wheel and for
hours and hours we sat in silence.

"Lily, we can't just keep sitting here.
I'm sorry if I was out of line."

"You weren't! You weren't out of
line! It's just that everything's crazy
right now Colbs."

"But I just wanted to make you feel
better. Lily, you're such a great girl
and you don't get it. You don't see
that I'm giving up a lot to help you.
I'm scared too. I've never stolen a
boat before, or put my life in danger
like this. We really don't know
what's going to happen. But I do
know that I'm willing to risk it for
you. I've never met anyone like you
before and I never want to lose you.
I'm sorry if what I did was bad

timing, but you need to know how I feel."

Honestly, what do I say to that? He's everything I've wanted and now he wants me.

"You don't know how much that means to me, Colby."

I just went over and kissed him again. Maybe that's all I needed to say, or do. I'm not exactly a wizard with words but I really did feel the same. What he was saying was what I had been dreaming of since I met him, and I was almost too shocked to respond.

Colby kissed me back excitedly. There were electric sparks passing through us and I knew that finally this was right. Even though we had a lot on our minds, what we were doing was right. It was meant to be; me and him.

I wasn't sure what was going to happen next, but I didn't have time to think about it, because suddenly our boat just came to a stop. We

were in the middle of the ocean,
nothing around us, yet the boat
would not go. Colby pressed the gas
and turned the wheel but for some
reason it was like our boat was glued
to the spot it was in.

"What the hell is going on Lily?"

"I don't know." I said with fear.

Chapter 20

Dear Revista,

Mom and Dad were nervous. We all knew this was coming but I don't think any of us were ready. They said the first thing to do was to round everyone up. The sun was rising as all four of us spread out along the island two by two, convincing others to join us and be ready for what was coming in the morning.

We knew that the Hadas were doing the same; gathering up in a mass to fight. And we knew that our time was limited.

Storm and I knocked on the doors of people's houses. I pleaded with these people who I'd known my whole life, against something I'd thought my whole life. It was strange really. I'd developed relationships with these people, all of us understanding that we loved where we lived and we loved the hadas that provided for us, but at that moment it was my mission to get them to stop believing that.

My parents had been talking to many of these people previously, so it wasn't like they weren't warned, but none of us actually expected this war to happen so quickly.

A lot of people were afraid. They had every right to be. But I've never seen someone convince a group of people like Storm did. His hazel eyes pleaded with them, and whether it was his good looks, his passion about the subject, or his overall friendliness, Storm was getting way more people to join in with us then I could have ever imagined. He even set up a meeting time earlier with my parents and got everyone to come to the crystal in the mid afternoon.

My parents on the other hand struggled more than we did. They went down to the market to try and convince others to come fight with us. The problem was that the hadas were extremely friendly with the market people, because they provided them with all of their supplies. The people didn't want to believe that the hadas would do such a thing, and every single one of them knew what they were capable of.

They worked hard but there was only so much they could do. We all understood that not everyone would be on our side, but we wanted to get our army as big as possible. We knew the hadas were powerful, after all we'd been dreaming for centuries so they were bound to have a lot of power. But, if I could outsmart them like I had when I rescued Storm, we could all work together and succeed.

"Storm, it's time to go back. We've knocked on countless doors and I'm tired. We need to rest up before this happens and get everything together. I want to see my parents, let's go home."

"Jade, you can't just give up this easily."

"I'm not! We've worked through the night and into the morning and there's only so much we can do. This is my home, Storm, it matters more

to me what happens to it than it does to you, and I think this is good enough."

"God, Jade, that's your problem. You've got an endless imagination that spans beyond my wildest dreams but sometimes your mind is so tight, so closed. You don't think about the rest of the world. You think you do, like you tell me that you want to travel, and you think about that, but what about what goes on in the world, Jade? What about the fact that my father died thinking I'd be able to save this place. What about the fact that people may die, or get injured, and your entire world is going to be flipped upside down because of me and my family. So, sorry if I care about what happens."

I would have never guessed that these words would come out of Storm's mouth. He was always gentle with me—sure we had our small fights—but he was never angry like this. And Storm was livid.

"Storm, I—"

"You don't have to say anything Jade, we need to focus on what's ahead of us."

"No, I want to. I want to say I'm sorry. That you're right. I've been pushing you away because I was so freaked out about what was going on with my home I didn't know how to react. But this is not just my home. It means more to you, maybe even more than it means to me. You see, I've always been saying that I wanted to get away and see the world, but you're the one that wanted to be right here. I'm fighting this battle for you Storm, not for myself, or for what I've known my entire life, but for you."

I hadn't looked up the whole time I was speaking, but after I was done, I saw tears dripping softly down his face. It wasn't the fearful sobs I'd seen before, this was a gesture to me that what I had said meant more to him than anything he could put in words. I didn't need words though. I just hugged him, and held him tight. We walked back to my house together, hand in hand. It was time.

Chapter 21

We'd been on the boat for a while before we hit it. And we were on the boat a while after we did.

At first, Colby checked to see if the boat was broken, if the engine had stalled, or if something like an anchor dropped. We had extra gas on the boat, which was definitely necessary, so we knew that wasn't the problem. The water sloshed around us and none of it made sense. Even if there was a broken engine or no gas left, the water should have moved us. We were floating, but it wasn't like it usually was, it was like we were being held down by a force.

I frantically paced the outer edges of the boat, looking for something. If what Jade wrote was true, and there once was fairies alive and flying around, then who knows what kind of magical creatures the world possessed. Maybe there was a sea monster holding us back, or holding us down.

"Lily, I need to show you something."

"What is it Colby? Am I going to be scared if I see it? Does it have teeth and claws?"

"What? No, just come here. It's the map, it's our location."

I peered over his shoulder and saw exactly what he did. We had passed Yucatan and according to Doug's plans, we were about a mile away from País de los Sueños. I ran to the front of the ship and looked out as far as I could. It was true, I could see a small line of land. I knew there was something there, I could make out an island, and at this point I was almost positive that it was the Lost Land.

"There's something keeping us from going there, Lily."

"I know. What is it? I can't see anything."

"Maybe it's not what we can see."

He ran to the front and reached his hand out. The strangest thing happened. It was like there was a wall of glass right in front of our boat because his hand stayed flat, like it couldn't go any further. He kept pushing and pushing but it wasn't going anywhere.

I ran up too. The same happened to mine. No matter how hard I pressed my hand it was stopped.

"We have to get through, Colby."

"Lily, I really want us to, but I don't see how we can! I'm not that strong and this thing is. Even our boat can't push through it."

I was stumped too. I searched left and right to find something. We started throwing things at it, anything we could find. Life jackets, wooden chairs, rope, but all of them just bounced back.

"Lily, over here!"

Colby was smiling next to the side of the boat. I ran over, thinking he found a loophole, but didn't see anything.

"Lily, look. There's a rowboat. Maybe whatever is keeping us away is in the air. If we get down low enough, we may be able to cross it."

I didn't really believe him, but I didn't have a solution, so I went along. We rowed up, but we were blocked again. We couldn't get through and we were in a small boat in the middle of a vast ocean, frozen in place.

"Colby, I'm scared. Let's go back."

"Lily, there's got to be a way. You're a legacy here, we can figure out how to get in!"

"No we can't! There's no way for me to prove to anyone that I'm welcome here, because there's no one here to even see us. Let's go back."

Colby sighed and started with the oars. The only problem was the boat wouldn't move. Whatever curse was in front of was now surrounding us. This time, Colby didn't have anything to say. I began turning the ring around my finger nervously, trying to distract myself, but it was no use. I just started crying and I couldn't stop. I looked out at the edge of the boat and saw the only view I would ever have of País de los Sueños, and it killed me. The tears rolled right from my eyes into the salty water below. I turned to look at Colby and he just hugged me. There was nothing more to do.

Suddenly he shoved me back. I was scared, I could see from his face we were in danger. I wasn't sure whether to look or not, but he kept pointing towards the island with a shocked look, and the water below us began to slosh faster. Finally, I turned around.

There was a man who started to appear from the invisible wall. It was crazy. I couldn't believe my eyes. He literally came out of nowhere, at least nothing that the naked eye could see, and slowly turned to look at us. His eyes were a deep green, majestic, and his whole body was glowing lightly, a purplish color, with a green merman tail making small splashes on the cusp of the water. I'd never seen such amazing eyes, or something so magical, I couldn't stop staring. This glowing man was appearing out of thin air but it was his eyes that stopped me. It was like they held a million secrets. They'd seen everything but they felt nothing.

"I'm sorry to report that you will die here."

That's all he said. The water whipped around us, faster and faster. Colby gasped, speechless. The man started to turn away, but I couldn't let him leave. He was glowing. He was part of the island, and so was I. I wanted to try and make him understand.

"Wait! Please wait! My mother is on that island. I need to go!"

I turned my ring nervously. Maybe it would channel some of her spirit, some of her courage.

"Please, my dear child. Your foolish games won't save you."

"Her name was Ariella. Her mother's name was Jade. Please, please give me a chance."

He turned and his eyes flashed. He looked at me, really looked at me, with those deep, green eyes. I stared up at him with a tear stained face, pleading that some how he could save us. I could see that what I was saying was convincing him, I knew I needed to keep going.

"Sir, my name is Lily. I grew up without a mom, and it's been really hard. Just a few weeks ago I found out that when she left me, it was to come here, to País de los Sueños. This is my one shot to find her, please help me."

"How do you know the name? How do you know this is País de los Sueños?"

"My mother left me this journal. It was Jade's, her mother."

"I know who her mother is. But how did you find us?"

"You know her?"

I couldn't believe it. She was a real person, and she was really on the island. My mother was one big piece of this magical and mysterious puzzle of the world.

"Jade had a map in her journal. If you want to see it, I can show you."

I started to reach for the book and his eyes darted to my hands.

"Stop. Your ring. I'd recognize it like it was my own. You really are Ariella's daughter."

For the millionth time that day my eyes started running. Tears were falling, but this time, they were happy tears. My mother was alive, and she was here, and he knew her, and now he knew me.

"Welcome to País de los Sueños."

As my ears tingled with those words I heard a sound, like a warp, and all of the sudden our small rowboat was being pulled toward the island. There was no longer an invisible barrier, nothing keeping me from my mom.

I turned to look at Colby and his face was in awe. I'd always needed him by my side when my courage came out, but right then I almost forgot he was sitting behind me. This was about me and my mom, and I'd do whatever it took to find her. Colby knew that. The pride in his eyes made it clear.

Suddenly the rowboat stopped moving and I looked up ahead of me. We'd hit land. This was it. This was País de los Sueños.

Chapter 22

Dear Revista,

We all decided to meet at the park. That's where the hadas would be and we knew we had to come on head on. Right before midday my family starting walking down, hand in hand. My parents tried frantically to assure us.

"We're strong. We'll be fine." My dad said.

"We can do this. Don't be scared Jade. Don't be scared Storm. It'll be okay." My mom assured us.

"We just need to get through this. We can defeat the hadas and we'll all live together. Happily ever after." My dad tried to continue on with the encouragement.

"Your father and I were just talking about how strong you both are. You can do this. And so can we. Together, we'll get through this. Please, believe in yourselves."

"It's not going to be easy, but it's for our home, Jade. Stay strong." My dad whispered.

I held Storm's hand tightly. He gripped mine right back. There was no convincing us, no filling our minds with words that would change our point of view. All four of us knew whatever was going to happen would be bad. In the end, it'd be the best for our home, but people were going to get hurt.

Everyone from my land came together for this. We knew we had to do it. I looked to my right, and to my left, and saw the solemn but determined faces of the people I'd known my whole life. We walked along the path in the park, and just as the tip of the crystal was coming into view, there was a light stronger than I'd ever seen. It was the hadas. They'd arrived.

They were flooding towards us, slowly. Almost as if they were warning us, giving us one final chance to choose to fight against

*them. We stood our ground, bracing
ourselves for the fight.*

    *I'm sorry Revista, but I can't
continue. I can't start talking about
this; I'm not ready. I'll write back
soon but I need to think of something
else, distract myself, and figure out
my life now.*

Chapter 23

It was just as beautiful as I had imagined. For years I'd read Jade's words but everything I'd been imagining was coming true. The flowers in all colors were so close I could touch them. The crystal clear water was lightly misting the air on the shore by the dock. The softly pale sand was blanketing the beach like velvet. The hot sun was shining down like magical rays feeding purity onto the island. It was so real; it was so right.

I didn't know where to start. She was on the island, I could feel it, but I didn't know where to look. The merman saw my shock and confusion and told me I should try looking in the market, she loved the market.

"Where is that?"

"Well, it's right around the corner. Go straight through the sand and you'll see a path. It'll take you through an area covered in trees, but you won't miss the market. You'll hear the hustle and bustle before you see it, but it's quite colorful. Enjoy."

He smiled and disappeared into the water. That man would remain a mystery, but one we couldn't worry about. My mom was walking the same land as me, it was my duty to find her. I started running towards the trees, trying desperately to see the path he was talking about. When I remembered Colby, I turned around looking for him. He was right behind me, panting but saying,

"Don't worry, I'll follow. Let's find her."

He couldn't be more perfect. He always knows what I want. When I want it. Well except for the kiss. But so what, everyone has flaws.

We found the path in the cool shade of the trees and followed it down a few yards. It was made of stone, but had clear rocks scattered inside. I wondered what that was. Suddenly, I started to hear the voices. It sounded like Times

Square, in the heat of tourism season, and I knew it was the market. I stopped.

"Colby, I'm scared. What if she doesn't remember me? What if she doesn't want to see me?"

"Lily, you're being ridiculous and you know it. I won't sit here any longer with you, I'm going to find her."

He grabbed my hand and lead me into the heat of the market. The mysterious man was right; the market was crazy. Luckily for Colby and I, we'd both been used to life in New York City. We knew how to handle ourselves.

He pushed through crowds as I scanned everyone's face. It was hard and we moved fast but I could see enough to know that she wasn't there. We needed to do something.

Colby lead me to a bread stand where there was a beautiful woman standing behind the register, arguing with a man about a price. He started to walk away and she looked up at us.

"Do I know you?" She asked me with a puzzled look on her face.

"No, you don't, but I need your help."

"I definitely do. I've seen you before. There's something so familiar about you."

"Well, then maybe you can help me. You may know my mom. Ariella? Do you know her?"

"Of course! Your eyes! They're a dead give away! You've got the same eyes as her, like a purply blue. I've never seen it before except with you two. Wow, Ariella has a daughter? Who knew?"

"Do you know where she is? Can you help me find her?

"Of course! She's probably at home right now! God, this explains so much! She'd been really distant since she went to America. I'm

Eden, by the way. My mother's name was Melinda, she knew Jade really well. Jade was such an amazing woman, but you probably already knew that. She's your grandmother for crying out loud!"

I didn't know Jade. I wish I could tell Eden that I did, that I could share her joy, but I didn't know her. This was so much harder then I thought it'd be.

"Excuse me, but my friend would really like to find her mom. I'm sure once we do, we can come back and chat, but it's kind of important we find her."

Colby to the rescue, once again. Could this boy do wrong?

"Oh, yeah I'm sorry! I'm being rude! Your mother lives on top of Estrella's Cliff, do you want me to show you where that is?"

Estrella's Cliff, where Jade and Storm first kissed. It was a real place, and my mother lived there.

"No, thank you but I have a map. Colby let's go! It was nice meeting you! Thanks again!"

"Yeah, no problem!"

But her voice was quiet as my mind started running a mile a minute. I grabbed Colby's hand and started running. I didn't need the map. I'd stared at it for years, stared at the spot where Jade had her first kiss. I knew it like the back of my hand. It was always so special to me, and now more than ever.

We climbed up to the top of the island and found the cliff. I saw the waves crashing gracefully, and felt the ocean mist on my face. And I saw a house. A small white house. With all of the vegetation around the island it really stood out because only one single type of flower surrounded it. Lilies. There were lilies covering the lawn, so many that there was just one narrow path to take to get to her house. The path was covered with the same clear rocks. I knew it was hers.

My feet froze. I couldn't do this.
I couldn't open that door, and see
what was behind it, because I was
too scared it would be
disappointment. There was a chance
she had a family here, a new one that
made her forget about my dad and I.

"Lily, no."

Colby picked me up and carried
me to the door. He just knew. He
always does. He put me down and
knocked. We just stared at each other
as we waited. My heart was beating
faster than a cheetah can run. It was
so surreal, I wasn't even sure what
was happening.

Slowly, the door started to open.
I closed my eyes, I didn't want to see
my mom's new husband answer the
door, wondering who these strangers
were. Colby grabbed me and I forced
myself to look.

Ariella was standing there. Right
in front me. Her face changed from
confused to flabbergasted. Her hair
was just like mine, long and wavy.
Dark brown, almost black, but

confined. Eden was right, her eyes were replicas of mine. The purple-blue, a color I'd never really identified to myself before. I guess my eyes were different, but I'd never noticed. They were something that we shared. Actually, I was almost a younger version of her. She knew who I was. I saw it process through her face. She reached out her hands to hold me and she was shaking like a leaf. I wasn't sure what to do either. Colby shoved me, and I walked into her arms.

It was as if I'd just put a key into a lock. As soon as I felt her in my arms I couldn't let go. We stood there, together, crying. I brushed my hand on her hair, the hair that was just like mine. This was my mother. I was hugging my mother. I couldn't believe it.

She pulled away and with tears in her eyes she looked at me. Those eyes, the eyes we shared, analyzed my own.

"Just let me look at you Ryan. Just let me take in your beauty."

I crumbled at her words. Her voice. It was beautiful. It was the new song to my soul, everything I needed. I was on the island where my ancestors were from and I was with my mother. Everything was perfect.

"Please, come in. I'm sorry I never introduced myself. I'm Ariella."

"Hi, I'm Colby. This is Lily, but you already knew that."

"Ah, so you chose your middle name? I kind of knew you would. I planted my flowers for you. They're lilies."

"I know. I'm sorry I'm Lily. If you want me to be Ryan, I'll be Ryan."

"Lily's such a pretty name. Ryan has meaning, love, but Lily is what you should be called."

"Meaning? What does Ryan mean?"

"Come inside, I'll explain it all."

She grabbed my hand and lead me into her house. My mother and I were holding hands, in her house. I looked around and it was exactly what I would have expected. She was free, and so was her lifestyle. There was moderate furniture but it was a house meant for the beach. That was her life, the ocean, the water, this island.

"Would you like anything? Water? Food?"

"No, all I need is time here with you."

She hugged me again and all three of us sat down in her living room. I couldn't believe it. My mother, my almost boyfriend, and I, sitting in País de los Sueños together.

"How in the world did you get here Lily? It's nearly impossible!" My mom asked.

"Nothing is stronger than a daughter's love Ariella. You should have seen her, she wouldn't give up. I have to admit, I was scared, especially when that man came out of nowhere and told us we were going to die," Colby proudly explained.

"Emilio? He's always trying to scare people, but don't worry, we're old friends. I guess he has to frighten people away; he can't let just anybody near the island. We can't have visitors here you know, it'd be too dangerous," My mom's voice was serious.

"Ariella, I mean… Mom, why do you keep saying it's dangerous?"

"I love the sound of that. Mom. It's so beautiful. There's a lot to explain Lily. I noticed the ring, I'm so happy you're wearing it. They'd be happy to, since it's their wedding ring," My mom smiled.

"Whose wedding ring?" I asked.

"My parent's. But you know all about them Lily, because I'm assuming you've read Jade's journal, since you've made your way here.

And Ryan was Storm's middle name."

"Storm is my grandfather? They really get married?"

"Yeah. I know the journal kind of ends on a bad note, but it turned out okay. Storm and Jade got married and had me! I was the only one, which was sad being the only child. I guess you know the feeling."

"Of being alone in your family? Yeah, I do." I lowered my eyes as I said this.

That was way too harsh. I shouldn't have said that. She started crying.

"Lily, please understand. I think of you every day. I've been taking care of my flowers like they were my own children, and I hate myself for leaving you. But you have to understand that I had to. Someone had to be in charge of the dangers here."

"Mom, what dangers? I don't understand."

"Well, you see, there's a chance of revival. Of the hadas. I can't really explain it right now, but after the war, my parents were put in charge of the safety of the island. When they passed, it was left to me. I wanted to bring you here, with your father, but I couldn't. If something were to happen, I would never forgive myself. I felt like I was locked in a cage here, trying to break free, free to the world that you lived in, but I couldn't."

My mother, the free-spirited Ariella, was trapped. She wasn't free like I thought; she was burdened by her role here. She was stuck like Colby and I had been in the boat.

"It's okay. Don't be sad, I forgive you. I'm here now and that's all that matters."

"You're right, Lily. I want to hear everything. Literally your life story from the day I had to go to the moment you got here. Same with you Colby. If you're a friend of my daughters, you're a friend of mine."

"Colby's not my friend, he's my boyfriend."

Why'd I say that? That wasn't true. He wasn't my boyfriend. Sure, he kissed me, and yes, I kissed him back, but so what? He's not my boyfriend. Ugh, I probably just ruined everything.

"Yeah, Lily's a special girl, Ariella. I'm just lucky to have her."

OMG. He didn't even act surprised. He just grabbed my hand, hinting that what I said was okay. I can feel the butterflies fluttering in my stomach. My life is a dream.

"Lily, I want to know about your dad. How is he? You can tell me if he has a girlfriend, or even a wife. I can take it. I just want to know he's happy."

"Ha, a girlfriend? No way! He's so caught up on you I can't even explain it. My whole life he's never had a date. I think he's always been waiting for you to return. He says that he focuses on being a dad, not a boyfriend, but secretly I think he knows he'll never find love the way he did with you. He's okay though. I don't know if you could necessarily say he's happy. Especially after all of this. To be honest, he didn't let me come here. I mean, I don't even know if he knows I'm here."

"Ryan Lily Dorlin! Please tell me you are joking. This is not okay. We need to contact him somehow, let him know you're safe. You two came here by yourselves? That's dangerous! Your father is fragile! You can't just leave him like that!"

She said it before she thought about it. But after, she realized. It got really quiet, and she looked down, like she was ashamed. I didn't want to say anything back. I wasn't going to sit here and blame her for leaving us, that just wasn't as important as getting to know her was. And she realized that she had no right to be playing a motherly figure when she hadn't been a mother for my entire life.

"Mr. Dorlin's pretty cool though. He tends to bounce back. Lily left him a note, and I'm sure he trusts her to be safe. I wouldn't worry."

"Lily, this is not good. I know I'm not one to talk, but I'm not happy you did this."

"But don't you understand Mom? It was all to find you! I had to!"

"I know, sweetie. I know. I really wish there was something I could do, but there's no way for me to contact him, and all I want to do is enjoy your company. Why don't you just stay the night, and we'll deal with this in the morning."

"Of course! But first, I want a tour of the island! I've already had a written one from Jade, but I want to see the real thing!"

"It would be my pleasure. You two are going to adore it."

My mother called Eden, and the two of them took us to all of the hot spots. The places that I'd read on the maps, the names my fingers had traced over and over. The words became real. Casara's garden was one of the most beautiful things I had ever seen in my entire life. Dad and I traveled, but never had I seen something as exotic as País de los Sueños.

Charriet's was still there, Mich's Montañas were tall and gave us a great view of the island, and La Playa De Greel was even more amazing than Jade had given justice. We sat in the sand there, the clouds rolled and thunder began to bang over us. Surprisingly, it was more peaceful that way. We just sat on the sand as rain started to fall and the sky boomed. There wasn't any lightening, so we weren't in danger, and I didn't feel for one second like I was. I just wanted to feel the thunder and the rain, the same rain that Jade had felt.

It got dark with the clouds and Ariella told us we had to go back.

She desperately wanted to take us to the park, but she said she wanted to see my face in the natural lighting when I got there. She said it would be better to see with the sun shining down.

The four of us started the hike toward her house, back to Estrella's and my mind was completely serene. For once in my life, everything was moving in harmony. I was beside my amazing boyfriend, the one that I'd secretly crushed on ever since I'd met him. And I was looking at my mother, the woman who I'd wondered about my entire life and idolized, though I didn't even know that much about her. She was everything I'd wanted her to be. Everything was just right. I smiled to the ocean view from her house until I heard,

"Steven, is that you?"

Yes, it was Steven. That was my father, sitting on Ariella's porch. Apparently, my mom explained to Eden while Colby and I were exploring that we had come behind the back of my dad. Eden had a feeling he wouldn't let me go that easily, so she told Emilio to look out for him. That he did, so my dad passed the barrier, and ended up here. Oh god.

Chapter 24

Dear Revista,

It's time I get this down on paper. I'm just going to write about what happened, but after that, I'm done. I can't keep sitting here, couped up in my room, writing down my feelings. It was fun while it lasted, but I have responsibilities now. I'm not ready for them, but I have to step up and overcome everything. The fate of my home is in my hands, just as it was before, and I won't let anything happen.

Within the first few minutes of fighting I witnessed a hada murder one of my friends that I'd known from the old school I went to. As I saw the light fade from her eyes, it hit me.

I had kept writing that I knew I had to accept that the hadas were evil, but it was hard for me. I thought I had accepted it before I'd started fighting, but when I saw the life run out of my old friends body, I really understood. They were terrible creatures out to hurt me. It didn't matter who I was, or how I thought of them, they didn't care who was in their way. They were murderers and they deserved the fight we were putting up.

A fire grew within my veins and I attacked. I fought for my people, my love, my family, and for my friend who lost her life. I wanted it all to be over, and I was willing to take part in anything that could make the process go quicker.

Revista, I want to make this clear. I am not proud of the violent actions that I committed during the battle. But I am proud of what I was fighting for.

My people fought unbelievably. None of us had ever had to deal with something like this, and I was surprised at how adaptable they were to the conditions. I guess none of us had time to think about it, we all just knew we had to get the whole thing over with.

I saw people I knew my whole life die right beside me as I fought off hada after hada. There were so many of them, I had no idea. They just kept coming, flying by with anger in their mystical eyes. It was something I thought I'd never see.

The first one I killed was the worst. It was a young hada, one who didn't know exactly what it was doing. I'm sure it wasn't the cause of the evil that was happening, and probably didn't affect the rest of them that much, but they sent it out to fight. It came up and attacked me, but I could see the fear in its eyes. I saw the vulnerability and pounced. I picked up a heavy rock and forced it into the hada's body, killing it on impact. I saw it look up at me, scared, like it didn't think I had it in me. Then its eyes shut, and it was gone.

I paused. I couldn't believe what I had done. I was a murderer. Just as bad as the hadas. But I had no time. Another hada came flying at me and I realized I wasn't as bad, because I wouldn't be fighting if it weren't for

them. They had to ruin the peaceful
life I was living. It angered me so
much that killing the next one was
easy, and simple. I used my knife for
my second murder.

I looked around and saw my
parents doing the same; fighting with
passion in their eyes. Then I saw in
horror Storm lying on the ground,
blood coming from his head. There
was a hada, laughing, as if they had
just told a joke, ready to kill Storm.
My mother and I made eye contact,
and she looked to where Storm was.
She saw it just as I did.

We both started sprinting over,
trying to save him. I took down the
hada and killed him harshly; I
wanted him to die. But it was no use,
another hada had flown in to finish
the job his peer could not. Mom tried
to fight him but he was strong. I went
over to help and grabbed him,
fighting. Mom screamed,

"Jade, do you love him? Do you love
Storm?"

"Yes, Mom, I do!"

"Then let's save him!"

She grabbed the hada and started strangling it. He didn't want to die, he wasn't ready. He started to strangle her back. I ran over, but it was too late. Both fighters had fallen dead. My mother died for Storm. He knew it.

I wanted the fight to end. I was done. I was exhausted. She was everything to me, and she was gone. So quickly, the hada didn't even feel sympathy. He'd stolen away my mother, and that was something I could never get back. My father became livid. The death didn't hit him with sadness, it hit him with anger. He killed hadas left and right, wiping out almost all of what was left of them.

There weren't that many of us left, but there weren't that many hadas either. We weren't giving up just yet, especially not my father.

Time passed, just as both hadas and humans did. Finally, there was

*just a few left, one of them being king
of the hadas, Pajana. He was always
a leader, the one to make the final
decisions in the group, and I knew he
was behind the plan they had.*

*He deserved the worst, but he
was strong. Really strong. I saw him
go after Melinda before I could
move. My dad and Storm also saw.
Storm knew that my parents loved
Melinda like their own, and my dad
couldn't afford to see another death.
I knew once it hit him that mom was
gone, his life would be over, and I
had a feeling seeing Melinda
murdered would trigger that. I had
to stop it.*

*Storm snuck up behind Pajana
and struck. Storm stabbed him, and
he shrieked with pain. He turned and
flew at Storm, attack him from
above. Storm was on the ground,
fighting for his life, when I jumped
in. I smacked Pajana hard with a
rock, and continued until I couldn't
feel my arm. He got really angry and
turned to fight me. Before I could
brace myself for the attack, Storm
grabbed hold of Pajana and brought*

him down to the ground. With one swift move, he plunged his knife into him, and Pajana whimpered as his body deflated into the ground.

We were all exhausted, not ready to fight any more, but they kept coming. I couldn't believe it. I was just done. I'd lost my mom, and in just a few hours I'd become a murderer. I couldn't go on like that, it wasn't right.

I saw the crystal sparkling across the battlefield and then looked all around me. All of my people were tired. We were strong, but I didn't know how much longer we could handle it. I thought about the hadas, and how my parent's kept saying that their power lay in the crystal's glow.

I didn't know what it would do, I didn't even really think about it, but I ran over with a huge stick and struck it. It was like slow motion. The stick contacted the surface of the crystal and I saw the hadas turn. There was a loud shattering noise, louder than I'd every heard, and a huge ray of light burst out from the shards and into the sky. The hadas faded until slowly they disintegrated into the ground. Everyone stared at me wide eyed, not knowing what to say.

I don't feel right. I may have saved the day, may have ended the war, but I ended the crystal. I stepped back and looked around at the remains, scattered all over the island, glistening in the sun.

My father came over and hugged me tightly. Then Storm came. The three of us stood in the park crying together for what seemed like hours. I just needed them to hold me, and they needed the same.

Where could we go from there? What could we do? We split apart and looked around us once again. Then I noticed my mother lying on the ground. After that, I fainted. I woke up in my room with a cold towel on my face.

Storm told me that I was okay, and that it would be okay. He told me the people cleaned up the

*battlefield and we were going to
have a ceremony in honor of our
dead loved ones that night. We were
to meet on La Playa de Greel and
send them away to the ocean. It
made sense, they all fought for their
homeland and died for their
homeland, so they would probably
want to remain here.*

*It all just felt like a dream. I
don't think I was able to comprehend
all of the deaths, especially not my
mother's. I kept thinking she'd come
by my bedside, and whisper
something warm in my ear. This
island is my family but with her gone
my whole world has changed.*

*She'd just been taken too soon.
It wasn't supposed to be like this at
all. We were just supposed to stop
the hadas, and win our lives back. I
should've hit the crystal earlier. I
could have smashed it sooner, and
then maybe all of the lives lost would
be here with us tonight.*

*Storm kept saying I couldn't
blame myself. My father tried to tell
me that I was actually the hero, not*

the problem, but I didn't feel like a hero at all. I felt like my whole body was being pulled down to the ground, even my eyes. The past few days were both physically and mentally exhausting.

I wasn't sure I would make it to the ceremony that night. It was both my fear and my mental state that would keep me away. In the end, I knew it was only right that I went. I had to pay tribute to those that I knew that I loved. I had to pay tribute to my mother.

Everyone hugged me on the beach. They told me they were sorry for my loss, and that they were still alive because of me. I couldn't believe these words being thrown into my ears. It wouldn't bring my mom back. They told me they missed her already, and tried to tell me how special she was. I know. I'll always know. I didn't need confirmation from others about my mother's perfections.

It may have been selfish for me to be angry with them. I realize they

*were just trying to help, but they
didn't understand my pain. They
knew her and loved her, but they
weren't her daughter. They didn't
know her like I did. They didn't love
her like I did. Like I do.*

*Everything's been gray since
then. The sun has not come out, and
the smiles have done the same.
We're slowly picking up the pieces of
what happened, coming to terms with
the deaths and the new lifestyles.
We'll have to work now, no more
hadas to supply for us. A lot will
change, Revista.*

*I wish I could write something
beautiful for my mother. Something
for my memories, something positive.
I'm just at a loss. She was an
amazing woman whose journey in
life was helping others. She
dedicated all of her time to ensuring
that our island thrived off of what we
could. And she was loving. After
years of marrying my father, she
loved him like every day was the
honeymoon. Her love for me was
unconditional. There is nothing more
powerful than a mother and her*

daughter, and I can gladly apply that to us. The love she possessed was stored inside the creases around her mouth from her constant smile, and the slight wrinkle by her eyes from squinting at the sun.

She was not just my mother, but the mother of this island, and today we remember her with appreciation.

She was taken too soon, but I could not be more thankful for the short time I had with her. I couldn't imagine having a bad relationship with my parents. Throughout my life they've been my rock and my father continues to fill that responsibility. We're strong, we're fighters, and we'll get through this.

Revista, it's time I go. I will now fulfill my mother's mission of keeping this island in one piece. My family is missing one, one we will never forget, but we will continue to spread serenity to our home.

I dedicate this book to the sunshine of my teenage years; my mother.

Chapter 25

Colby and I left them alone. Just like when I'd first seen my mom, I had a lot to say, to ask, to hear. I'm sure my dad did the same, and I knew they'd want to talk privately so I walked Colby to the edge of the cliff at Estrella's. It was perfect really. I forgot my dad would be angry with me when I was sitting there with Colby. Though he hadn't read it as many times as I had, he knew the story of Estrella's. The tragic love story creating the stars in the sky, and that curse bringing a charm for couples ever since. We laid in the grass, my head on his chest, and I just listened to him breath.

In the city you can't see the stars because of all of the pollution and lights from the skyscrapers. I once lived in Montana, and I saw the stars there, but we only lived there for six months and I was young then. Other then that, I'd been in cities, and since Colby's lived in New York his whole life, he'd never seen anything like this. They were so bright they illuminated the water and you could still see ripples from fish below the surface. Colby and I stared at the stars while he stroked my hair and my head bobbed to the rhythm of his breath. Slowly my eyes started to close.

I woke up to the sun brightly shining and I looked around, confused. It took me a second to realize where I was. And whom I was with. With Colby, my mother, and my dad.

My dad. We had to find him. I couldn't avoid him for long, it was time to go in and see my parents. Wow, I can't believe my parents were in the same country, the same room even.

I shook Colby and his eyes lit up when he saw me. He lazily smiled and then looked around, just as confused as I was.

"You thought this was a dream didn't you?"

"Yup. Except in my dream, we jumped off the cliffs like your grandma and grandpa and swam until the end of the world where it was just you and me."

"That sounds really nice right about now, especially since we have to go inside and face my dad."

"Or, we could stay out here and let the sun take over our bodies. C'mon, let's go back to sleep."

I kissed him lightly on his velvet soft lips and grabbed his hands, pulling him to his feet. He sighed and draped his arm around me as together we headed to the house.

We opened the door to the smell of fresh food. I heard the tea kettle steaming loudly which lead us to the kitchen. My mother was smiling at the stove.

"Come on in guys! Breakfast will be ready in about five minutes. You can have a seat at the table until then!"

"Good morning mom. Thanks for the breakfast."

"No problem. You two are so cute! After your dad and I talked we came out to find you and you were sleeping in the grass. I wasn't sure whether I should wake you but your dad and I both agreed you two were too peaceful to disrupt. Young love! You were like a picture out of my mom's journal!"

We both smiled. This whole couple thing was still new to us, and it warmed every ounce of the blood in my veins to have a picture of Colby and I resting at Estrella's in my head.

"Thanks for the breakfast, Ariella. This is a beautiful home, we're so happy to be here."

"No need to be polite Colby. I'm happy to have you guys!"

"Is Dad up yet?"

"Nope. I'm an early riser but your father was always one to sleep in late. He used to say, 'If I love my sleep then it's not a waste of the day, it's an efficient way to spend my time.' I never agreed, the most important things happen in the morning. Life just flashes before your eyes, you know?"

"Definitely. Is there any way you could point me in the direction of the bathroom? I have to go."

"Sure Colby, it's right down that hallway on the right."

"Thanks!"

Colby left swiftly and finally it was just my mom and I.

"Is he really mad at me?"

"No, I wouldn't say he's mad. He was worried that he'd lose the only girl he had left, though. But I calmed him down, Lil. I guess I'm just so happy to have both of you here, I don't really want anything to ruin this."

"Wow, thanks. I would say I don't know how you calmed him down but I know how much he admires you. You could probably tell him to run around the island three times screaming 'I LOVE ARIELLA' and he would."

She started laughing. Her laugh was so pretty. It was light, nothing heavy. She didn't have a weird snort or a loud cackle, just a fluffy giggle. My mother was everything I ever wanted to be. I hope I can grow up to be like her some day.

"Mom, I have a question. You never finished telling us about the dangers that are here. Should I be scared?"

As I asked that my dad groggily padded into the kitchen. She kissed him and laughed as she said,

"No, you shouldn't be scared. Don't worry about it."

So my mom just kissed my dad. Should I be confused or excited? I know this is so normal for a million people in the world but it was one of the weirdest things for me.

Colby came back from the bathroom and smiled at my dad. It was like a picture of a perfect family. We were on a beautiful, exotic island, my mom and dad lovingly looking at each other and my boyfriend gingerly holding my hand at the breakfast table. The sun was shining and I couldn't have been happier. My dad came and sat down with us as we all awaited our breakfast.

"So, how'd everyone sleep?"

"Surprisingly good for being on the ground."

"Yeah, the waves were pretty calming."

"I always find that sound to be one of the most soothing in the world. Maybe because I'm from here, but it just puts me at ease. Did you guys have good dreams?"

"My dream was lovely."

Colby said, smiling at me. I knew why he was so happy, and it made me even happier.

"What about you Steven, did you dream of something amazing?"

"I don't need to dream, everything I want is right here in this room. Besides, I never dream. I don't know why, it's pretty weird, but I just can't get myself to do it."

My mother's face went white and she dropped her spatula on the ground. I heard the clatter and saw her stand there, frozen in place. My heart started to run and I grabbed Colby's hand. I didn't know what was wrong, which scared me even more. I smelt the eggs burning and the tea kettle got louder and louder. Everything else was a blur.

She ran to the table and started yelling,

"Steven, you're not being serious, are you? You had a dream, you have dreams. You have to have dreams."

"Ariella, what's wrong?"

She ran to the window and looked outside.

"Mom, what's going on? Please, tell us!"

"Lily, Colby, Steven, you have to get out of here. You have to leave, now."

"Mom, what is happening?"

"Please, follow me. I'll explain on the way, but we have to go."

Hurriedly she raced out the door and we all followed. No one was sure what was going on except her, so, naturally, we were all extremely worried. Almost in a line we raced past the coastline, the trees, the flowers. She was screaming,

"This was the danger. The hadas had been weakened by those that couldn't dream, but when my mother smashed the crystal the role was reversed. Our dreams weaken them. Even though it seems like they don't exist, their souls are trapped in the clear rocks you see. Those rocks are pieces of the crystal. Lily! Quick! Rip off that ring! Get it off! Throw it away! Get it away from you! There's pieces of the crystal on it, you can't have it"

I didn't want to let go, but she was so frantic I had no choice. I started crying and placed it in my pocket, I wasn't about to lose it.

"If someone can't dream, the hadas will gain back some of their power. If they come back, they'll be here to stay. It's not going to be that easy to get rid of them, we don't have a crystal we can smash. They'll figure out a way to get power and we'll all be doomed. That's why Emilio is so strict with visitors, why we keep our location hidden. We couldn't let strangers on the island because if someone came who couldn't dream, well…"

Then my father started crying. He kept muttering,

"Oh my god. We're all going to die and this is my fault. This is all my fault. I should have never come. I should have let her leave me, I don't deserve them."

We continued to run through the island and I paced myself next to him,

"Dad, don't say that. It's okay, you didn't do this on purpose. Maybe they won't come back. Please don't say that. You deserve us, we love you."

I don't know if I could be heard through my tears flowing into my mouth. Colby was scared. He squeezed my hand tightly and when we made eye contact I could see it in his eyes.

Then my mom screamed. She stopped, dead in her tracks on the sand, and her knees buckled until she was kneeling down. I looked to where her eyes had wandered. Out by the rocky area, something was happening. There were whispers of glowing air rising from the clear rocks. As we stood together on the beach, the four of us were frozen with shock because we all understood. The hadas were returning.